MAD MAN OF THE MOUNTAIN

Gothic Classics

MAD MAN

OF

THE MOUNTAIN.

A TALE.

TWO VOLUMES IN ONE.

BY

HENRY SUMMERSETT.

"Whither are fled the charms of vernal grace,
And joy's wild gleams that lighten'd o'er thy face?
Youth of tumultuous soul, and haggard eye!
Thy wasted form, thy hurried steps I view:
On thy cold forehead starts the anguish'd dew,
And dreadful was that bosom-rending sigh!"

COLERIDGE'S MONODY.

Kansas City:
VALANCOURT BOOKS
2012

Mad Man of the Mountain by Henry Summersett
First published in 2 vols., London: William Lane, 1799
First Valancourt Books edition, 2012

ISBN 978-1-934555-23-1 (*trade paper*)
ISBN 978-1-939140-02-9 (*cloth*)

Published by Valancourt Books
Kansas City, Missouri

Composition by James D. Jenkins
Set in Dante MT

10 9 8 7 6 5 4 3 2

CONTENTS

NOTE ON THE TEXT

THE Valancourt Books edition of *Mad Man of the Mountain* follows the text of the only edition of the novel, the first edition published by William Lane at his Minerva Press in London in two volumes in 1799. The division between the two volumes has been preserved for this edition, as has the drop-title for each volume, which in the original edition adds the word *"The"* to the title.

The 1799 edition poses few difficulties for an editor, as it contains very few errors of spelling, punctuation, or grammar. This edition follows the original text verbatim with no attempt having been made to modernize or standardize spelling or punctuation or to improve the grammar. Like most novels of its time, *Mad Man of the Mountain's* use of quotation marks is not always consistent or correct by modern standards. However, no attempt has been made to correct or regularize their usage, although in a couple instances, a stray mark has been removed, or a missing one added where necessary for clarity.

I could find nothing written about this novel, aside from the contemporary reviews reprinted in the back of this volume. Modern scholars seem to have ignored both it and its author. The few facts I have been able to discover about Henry Summersett are included in the Valancourt edition of his 1801 novel *Martyn of Fenrose; or, The Wizard and the Sword*.

James D. Jenkins
August 8, 2012

THE

Mad Man of the Mountain.

CHAP. I.

SO! the storm is past; the elemental warfare over; the thunder hushed; the lightning faded; and the winds have done their works of fury, and are satisfied!—I was told that I was mad to brave the tempest; that the fires of heaven would scorch me; and that the blasts would send me, headlong, from the mountains to the vallies.—"How!" said I; "are not the innocent under the protection of the Divinity? Favoured, cherished, supported? Can any of you accuse me of crime, of lust, of cruelty, or of murder? No! you know me not; I was not bred among you; I have formed no fellowship with you; reposed no secrets in your bosoms. You know not what I am; but, as I am, to the care of Heaven I confidently resign myself."

The peasants looked earnestly at me; the children hid themselves behind their mothers, and I went forth to meditate.—But who could calmly connect his thoughts in an hour like that? I could only look around me: the vineyards were destroyed; the grain rooted; the huts of the fishermen shattered; and, looking over a rock, I saw a vessel dashed in pieces! I heard the cries of mariners, the shrieks of women—I saw them perish!—Oh, what ruin!—How wonderful that so poor an insect as myself should escape it! I wandered till the convulsions of Nature subsided, till the sky looked smiling, and the waves were less boisterous. The peasants were then abroad, and the children, no longer fearful of the storm, had entered into their sports. Rose-lipped innocents! If any of you are doomed to know the miseries of Roncorone, happier had it been if such had perished amid the tumult of nature!

Weary—wretched and weary! Is nature never to be subdued by the means which I exercise? I expose myself to heat and to cold: summer produces no fevers, winter no agues; neither dews nor fogs can affect my body; and if I lie all the night on the damp earth, in the morning my limbs feel no contraction. Strange insensibility!

I will argue with some philosopher on the protraction of a miserable life: I once talked of it to a grey-beard, who called himself a sage, but we could not agree in principles. He had never known misfortune; he was a vehicle moved by few passions; and, in directing me to a road for which I had enquired, he sent me into a labyrinth. Smiling at his dissertation, he frowned on me, and said I was mad; but he was a liar! I was not then mad; my brain, indeed, has since been rent asunder, pressed, distorted;—and yet, even now, I can beat down his hypothesis, and prove that his arguments had more sound than reason.

Shame on such empiric philosophers! Hearken, you ragged herdsmen! leave awhile your goats, and remember the names which I shall repeat to you; speak of them with a grave face and solemn tone, and the world shall worship you. The fellow flies from me!—Rot in obscurity, then, and let not the word *great* be found in your epitaph.

It is strange that in this immense world I can find no society, or establish any friendships; man, woman, and child disclaim me, look on me with terror, fly from me. If I speak of my sorrows, it must be to the elements, or to some inanimate or senseless object; the miseries of Roncorone are confined to his own breast, and no one commiserates his sufferings. Is there on the earth so forlorn an object, so solitary a being—one so lost to the felicities of society, and to the joys of existence? I have of late had little commerce with man.—I have almost forgotten him; his virtues pass from my brain, and his good qualities are scarcely remembered, though I retain a sense of all his imperfections and vices. In the public haunts, he will assemble, converse, listen, and communicate; it is then that strife is nursed on the bosom of tranquillity. Even in these wild scenes, at the evening hour, I often see two fellow-labourers wind though the valley towards their little huts; their toil is over; their wives, their children await them; they are happy; they sing, and the mountain caverns echo their joy. Those who, in the frozen North, never thank the sun for its blessings, and those who, in the torrid zone, often gasp beneath its rays, still have their social pleasures. Let it be so; and God increase their happiness, though I am left to solitude and anguish! My imagination sometimes peoples my cell; on one side of me sits Misery, on the other Affliction; Despair groans at my feet; and, in the darkest recess, I see the fiery eye-balls of Insanity.—Congenial associates! reign unmolested till the broken voice of Death shall cry aloud, "Mortal, I summon thee hence; resist not my decree, but go with me into perpetual darkness!"

He is, however, a physician skilled in every malady, and yet the extent of his practice will not gain him reputation; let him only lay his bony fingers on the pulse, and you shall hear the terrified patient implore him to retire. Not so with me: I would see him for his art, and endeavour to make his name pass current as that of an able graduate;—he has hitherto avoided me; but he will soon be at the cell of Roncorone. On his arrival he may pronounce my distemper mortal; therefore, ere he approaches, I will employ myself in an office—I will go though the narrative of my life. It shall be laid in a corner of my cave, in order that it may be known by the villagers who the poor wretch of the mountain was. Most men who write their own lives, are stimulated by egotism:—what a fine polish do they give to their self-acknowledged virtues, and how curiously do they compress the story of their vices! They attach good motives to the basest of their actions; and the mere duties of fellowship are called ebullitions of sensibility and refined philanthropy. These schoolmen often puzzle us in finding their meaning. They have a general opinion, that sublimity must be obscure, lest the aptness of little minds should destroy the admiration of great ones.

To know that a man is virtuous, is sufficient to make us esteem him; but when he is allied to us, when our blood owes its source to him, and when to God and to him belong our very lives, we are inclined to exclaim, with mingled joy and pride, "This is our father! this is our father!"

So have I, a thousand times, and with the greatest fervour, said of my parent, whose uncorrupted soul, irreproachable manners, and virtuous habits of life made him the admiration of many, and also the envy of some. His ancestors had been the followers of Glory: he had, himself, trod in her paths, snatched laurels from her field, and been applauded for his valour and enterprise. These exploits had been performed in the vigour of youth and early days of manhood; but, marrying at the age of twenty-five, the solicitations of his wife removed him from the army, and established him in Venice, where I was born and educated.

He could not boast of the favours of Fortune; and love, not interest, had united him to my mother, whose property was inconsiderable;—but her personal charms were conspicuous, and her virtues more to be prized than a crown of pearls. As the dissipations of life were not by either of them considered as necessary to happiness, but were justly held to be the destroyers of it, they lived in retirement, and nicely limited their expenditure, in order that, in the days of age, there might be no complaints of insufficiency: to many, therefore, they were not known; still they had friends who were sensible of their worth, and even willing to proclaim it in society.

It was two years after their union before my mother gave me to the arms of my father, and bade him bless his God for me.— She nurtured me at her breast, reared me as a botanist would a tender plant, and at the age of five years I gambolled around her, her blooming, healthful, and darling boy!

The lives of my parents were tranquil as summer days; in them was seen the harmony of connubial affection, and a sweet accordance of sentiment and passions.—Their little Francesco was their delight;—and he was alternately in the arms of the one, and in the lap of the other. My father, when I was six years old, began to educate me; my mother also became my tutoress, and the manner in which I received their joint instructions, spread the faces of both of them with the smiles of pleasure and expectation. I was proud of the praise they bestowed on me, and, as I grew older, strove most sedulously to merit it;—a squeeze of the hand, or an embrace from my father, and a kiss from the lips of my dear mother, always rewarded my efforts; and to obtain either, young as I then was, I could have spent hours in striving to deserve them.

I was filial before I knew the signification of the word duty; and so much did I love my parents, that I believed no other man could be so noble and just—no other woman so good and virtuous. In my simplicity I told them so, and it made them smile: they attempted, however, to explain to me the error of my opinion, and to point out examples; but nothing that they said could convince me to the contrary, or correct the youthful ideas of their infallibility.—I still continued to grow, to learn, and almost to adore my parents; but a large portion of my happiness was lost to me, because it was evident that the health of my father was rapidly declining. I was the first to speak of the circumstance when he confessed himself ill; magnifying the malady when my mother was not present, I expressed to him all my fears and apprehensions, and his sickly smiles in these moments only served to increase my suspicions and distress.

For several months afterwards I secretly observed the effects of the disorder, which was now become chronical; the paleness of his cheeks, the feebleness of his voice, and the means which he used in order to conceal his pain, were all visible to me; and I doubted not but that the grave would soon hide him from me and my dear mother.

One evening he said to me—"I confess there are grounds for your fears, though I have been anxious not to shew them to you and to your better parent. I can counterfeit no longer. How old are you, dear boy?"

"In June I shall be thirteen, father."

"I shall not live till then!"—He sighed deeply.

"Not till then!" I cried; "not live till then—till June!—a very few months.—Oh, God grant that you may! God grant it!"

"Dear son!" said my father, "be composed, and do not let your mother hear you. You have ever been the best of children:—when I am dead, my boy—nay, if thus you weep and afflict yourself——"

"I will no more—go on—proceed, father."

"When I am dead, Francesco, let not your affection for your surviving parent ever decrease; solace, cherish, comfort her! she will much want your assistance."

"She shall have it! she shall have it!"

"I shall not leave either of you rich, but you will both be removed from want; the occurrences of life, however, are many and uncertain; should any disaster befal your mother——"

"I will take it to my own account; work from morning till night for her, and if she fall into affliction, I will not go from her bed till she is either restored to health, or removed from me by death for ever!"

My father pressed me to his heart; swept away my tears as well as his own, and would not suffer me to speak any more on the subject. He daily grew worse; my mother was almost frantic; I gazed on him with increasing anguish; his struggles agonized me nearly as much as himself; and, as he had presaged, *before June* I saw him on his death-bed! *before June* his body was laid in the burial vault of his forefathers! I strove not to conquer my emotions; my heart was bursting; and I was ever running to my mother, hiding my head on her bosom, and bewailing the death of my father.

Her conduct was such, that I had hopes I should not soon have to lament for her in a similar manner; she often wept, but, at the same time, strove to rouse me into activity. At first I thought her sense of feeling less acute than mine, and that she would forget the departed sooner than I should; but, Oh! I found, soon afterwards, that she smiled merely to comfort me; that she talked with an appearance of calmness on mortality even when the subject chilled her blood; and that the strings of her poor heart were each moment breaking.

She struggled six or seven months firmly: I then followed her to a sick bed—I then remembered the vow that I had made to my father; and, as I kissed her withering hand, repeated it. Days and weeks I hung over her; if I found her chilly, "She is dying!" I would exclaim, "she is dying!" But if a hectic came upon her cheeks, unskilled in the causes, and mistaking the effect of it, I would cry, "She will survive! My mother will rise again in health!"

The suggestions of hope, however, were false; for as I, one night, and at the latest hour of it, was gazing on her face, I saw it suddenly become convulsed and distorted; her extremities were cold and lifeless, and her eyes stedfastly fixed on me. I shrieked; rang a bell for some person to come to me; and, though stricken with terror, raised her in my arms, and begged her to let me hear her voice. Her mouth was twisted; but she strove to speak, and my ears caught the faint sounds of "God," and of "dear son." She fell agonized from my embrace, stretching to her greatest length; and her soul, aided by the spirit of immortality, soared to the regions of bliss and eternity!

Father! mother! the smiles of the Divinity and his angels, and all the blessings of the mysterious world, fall upon and encompass you!

I was now an orphan: my protectors, my instructors were gone; and my young eyes saw only desolation before them. The servants, who were in the house, joined their lamentations with mine, and with me sighed over the corpse of my mother. I had ever dearly loved my father;—had been conscious of his loss, and held him most faithfully in my memory; but when I attended the body of my other parent to the receptacle of death—when I saw her consigned to the cold earth, and knew that her eyes would open on me no more—that her tongue could no longer call me to her presence, and that her arms were never again to encircle my neck—I shuddered, groaned, and fell swooning into the arms of the second mourner at the funeral.

This person was Vincent Roncorone, the brother of my father, to whose care and protection my last surviving parent had consigned me. My uncle possessed fewer sensibilities than myself, or, possessing them, knew better how to conceal them;—he was a Professor of Philosophy in Venice; and those who attended his school were soon made acquainted with the hypotheses of the ancient stoics. Vincent, however, was not without tenderness, and in many cases his humanity was exemplary; his reputation was great as a scholar, and his followers in Venice were numerous.

He and my father had ever shewn a true fraternal affection towards each other; though their pursuits in their early years had differed materially, the bond of their love had never been broken; and when the one retired from the army to quiet life, the other courted his society, and was daily in his company. Vincent esteemed my mother as much as he did his brother; and, by the notice he took of me, it was evident that I was no inconsiderable favourite. The resemblance which he bore to my father alone caused me to

love him; and, in his conversation, there was something so pecu-
liarly striking, even to a young mind—at least to mine, that I abandoned the trifling pursuits of pleasure and amusement, merely to
hear him talk with my father on subjects which I could, however,
but little understand.

Still there was an inimitable tone, a manner, a gesture;—I listened, and sometimes thought I comprehended, and one day was
so fixed, that when he ceased to speak, and I went up to my mother,
who was sitting at some little distance, I found that my posture had
been sufficiently determined to enable her to draw a perfect resemblance of my face, and to give to it the expression of admiration
which had been actually stamped upon it.—From that happy to
this most miserable day, have I retained this token of her love and
genius; in all my vicissitudes, in all my troubles and distractions
retained it! And was I really once the boy it bespeaks—blooming,
joyous, animated? Now, whenever I bend over the stream, I see
reflected a deathlike figure; a resemblance of a pining ghost; a
sallow, miserable wretch!—And this is Roncorone: he from whom
every little innocent of the village flies to its mother, crying, "He
comes! he comes! Save me! save me!"

But I have been wandering from the paths of narrative.—My
uncle bore me in his arms from the grave of my mother; and when
my reason returned, I found him pensively hanging over me. I
instantly remembered my recent situation; I raised my head, and
laid it on his breast; threw my arms around his neck, and, sobbing,
exclaimed, "Oh my mother! my blessed, blessed mother!"

"She is blessed," said Vincent, placidly; "the finest feeling that
will ever enter into your soul while on earth, must be gross to
those which attach to the heaven-ranging spirit of your mother.
Francesco, dry up your tears: you are not a child; you have a mind;
plant in it fortitude."

"I cannot, uncle," I replied, "so soon wish to destroy the image
of my mother.—She was all tenderness: she had a thousand
virtues!"

"She has now a thousand rewards, nephew. The scale of
Omnipotence has already turned in her favour."

"Her former affection, at this moment, steals upon my soul.—

How she fondled me in my childhood! How she smiled on me in my sports! How she, in my growing youth——"

"Francesco, dismiss these thoughts if you would be happy. Think of your mother as a *saint*—forget her as a *woman*."

"I cannot forget that I am an orphan! I cannot forget that I have no friend on earth!"

"Francesco!" said Vincent, "in what character do you regard me? When your mother, on her death-bed, gave you over to me, do you think that *she* did not consider me as your friend?"

"Dear uncle!" I exclaimed, "forgive me; I have been rash; my grief has made me inconsiderate. But hear my apology, my justification."

"My affection can dispense with it," he replied: "only when we meet again, let me see you more tranquil. Be sure of this—if I can establish your happiness, improve your fortune, or enrich your mind, my assiduities shall never be wanting."

I bowed upon his hand, and he retired; I saw him again at night, when I affected to be more composed; and during several successive days, endeavoured to appear tranquil, though I had a load of grief on my mind. Vincent was apparently pleased with the alteration; he repeated his arguments on fortitude and stability, and put some books in my hand, which seconded his doctrines.—I read them partly, but they did not convince me; and laying them aside, I still thought there was a luxury in sighs and tears, though Vincent and the philosophers derided them.

Time softened my grief; and six months after my first residence in the house of my uncle, he declared my conduct to be just as he wished it. The images of the dead, however, were not cast down in the temple of my soul, nor had memory discarded them. Vincent Roncorone entered me as one of his pupils, and likewise gave me many private instructions; for he perceived that my understanding was naturally good, and was careful in improving and embellishing it as much as possible. We read and conversed together: such of his precepts and opinions as I admired, I treasured in my mind; but such of them as I disapproved—and at the age of sixteen I flattered myself that I possessed some powers of discrimination—I rejected and forgot. My first declamations were praised; when I was seventeen they were admired, and said to be wholly without puerilities, and I was by many called a youth of great promise. I had friends who assured me of patronage; I visited the Convents, and formed connexions with men of early and of advanced years; with the women I was not unacquainted; being no pedant, I talked not of books when in their company, and was generally called by them the agreeable Roncorone.

Oh days of happiness! I scarcely dare let my memory, even for one poor moment, dwell on ye. Were it then thought or suspected that I should irrecoverably lose the favour and opinion of the world? That man should hate, and reason forsake me?—But who can assure himself of a particle of felicity a moment beyond the one in which he actually enjoys it? Angels have been expelled from Heaven—man from the bowers of innocence—Emperors hurled from their thrones to drag the chain after the chariots of conquerors—and Roncorone—Oh misery and madness! * * * * *

* * * * * *

Vincent beheld my progress with pleasure, heard me praised with delight, made me the subject of his conversations, and treated me with an affection that filled me with love and gratitude. His mind was firm, but not austere; he even sacrificed to the Muses, and encouraged the talent he found I possessed for poetry; but he forgot not to speak of the general disappointments, the mortifications, and the miseries of those who place their hopes of fortune and advancement on their powers of versification. We did not often put reciprocal sentiments into metrical dress; his verses were generally philosophy harmonized; my stanzas were less saturnine, and I seldom left the epic paths but to step into those of love; nay, I accustomed myself so much to the latter walk, that my uncle at length threatened to take my pen from me, lest the indulgence of so soft a subject should sap the energies of my mind.—Vincent! thou canst not see me *now*.—My mind—my mind!——

My uncle had never been married; never had much converse with women; never knew, never would acknowledge the ecstacies of love; the passion so called he confined to friendship, beyond which he would not allow the sober soul to stray. This point I always warmly debated with him; our energies were nearly equal;

and when we closed on the subject, we found that the one had not, in any degree, influenced the other; we were both combatants, both victors.

I had entered into my twenty-first year, when a pestilential fever raged in Venice; hundreds of mortals were swept away in a day; and it seized, most furiously, my friend and monitor. It was soon visible that its effects on him were fatal; for he became enfeebled, his blood boiled, his face was livid, and his eyes retired far into their sockets. Reason was entirely annihilated; he raved, and died frantic in my arms.

Vincent! friend! father!—Even now the remembrance of thee draws tears from the eyes of Roncorone.

I attended him during the whole of his illness, raised him in my arms, wiped his forehead, and moistened his parched lips.—I was told that I should imbibe the infection, still I did not quit him; I thought of no danger, and resolved not to leave him till his breath was wholly suppressed. Could I then have foreseen the events which were dependant on my life, or a thousandth part of the miseries which have since fallen on me, I would have pressed Vincent closer to my breast; every noxious breathing that came from his body should have entered into mine. I would have sought the hospitals, and strained the foaming lazar in my arms till we had both madly died together.

I buried Vincent.—While I hung over his grave, my sufferings were almost as poignant as those which I experienced at the interment of my mother; and the torch-bearers seemed to behold me with terror as I stalked through the long aisle of the church in which he was laid. I found that all the philosophy of the deceased had not made me a philosopher. In his escritoir I discovered his will, which had been made some considerable time; and he had bequeathed all his property to his dear nephew, Francesco Roncorone, whom he prayed the Father of Heaven eternally to bless. With what rapture must the associating spirits have received such a soul as Vincent's!

My uncle had accumulated a considerable sum of money, and also managed my little fortune, during my minority, with such care, that I was surprised at my own riches. I had not entered into active life, nor did I feel inclined to do so after the death of Vincent. Some of my most intimate friends would talk to me on the subject:

I was much urged to follow the pursuits of my late uncle; but this I peremptorily declined. A gloomy Monk, of the Order of Saint Francis, invited me to join the brotherhood; and a lively Sicilian Officer held out many specious lures in order to draw me into the army. I inclined neither to bigotry nor to superstition; the oratory of both parties, therefore, might have been spared.

My name was not so much mentioned in Venice as it had been, and many people censured what they called my indolence; but, though I declined in the opinion of the men, I rose in the estimation of the women. I attached myself to the sex; they softened and polished my manners, and likewise refined my sentiments. I was invited to every party of festivity, and the women consulted me on many occasions: I selected books for some of them, and music for others; my opinions directed them in their studies, and my taste was deemed to be of a superior nature. Though my application in knowledge was not so intense as it had been, still it was not abandoned; and though I was less austere in my disposition, and more attached to pleasures, yet I shunned the profligate, the idle, and the ignorant. Those who thought my philosophy weakened, acknowledged that my poetry was improved; and I was now more ambitious of being thought to possess a beautiful imagination than a great and solid one.

My love for the sex to which I had then recently attached myself, was of a general nature, till I met with Rosolie Venzone.—Rosolie! What, write of Rosolie! Let me think.—Thought makes me mad!—Rosolie!—answer me—speak to Roncorone—Rosolie, Rosolie!—Ah! wherefore do I call on one long since stiffened by the hand of murder! * * * * * *

* * * * * * *

Spirit of Vincent! witness that I am a philosopher: for while the fiend urged me to leap the gulph of damnation, I named to him the power that had cast *him* into it—cursed him—fled! Was not that right, guardian of my youth? The focus of the mind again receives the rays of reason, and the aberration of ideas is over; they collect and associate.

I formed an acquaintance with a young German, whose name

was Alberti, and was by him introduced to many families, to which I had before been a stranger. I accompanied him one evening to the assembly of a female relation: there was a numerous company, and festivity ruled the hour;—many of the women were extremely handsome; but Alberti pointed out one to me, as possessing a great superiority of beauty; I looked at her, and not only confessed, but also felt, the truth of his observation.

She was young, exquisitely formed; her grace was unstudied; her charms natural; her eyes spoke sweetness of mind, and sensibility dawned from them. I thought she excelled every woman that I had ever seen, and equalled any one that I had poetically imagined;—I could not withdraw my observation till she looked at me; I then hurried to Alberti, who had left me, and urged some questions respecting the stranger. He smiled at my warmth; told me that her name was Rosolie Venzone; that her beauty was greater than her fortune; that she was an orphan, and had been left to the protection of Signor Salvini, the friend of her deceased father.

"Salvini!" I exclaimed; "what, Michael Salvini, who lived formerly at Florence?"

"The same," replied Alberti; "do you know him?"

"No."

"Do you *wish* to know him? I have some acquaintance with him, and will introduce you."

"No, no! Salvini and Roncorone can never be friends."

"Indeed!" cried Alberti; "how so, pray?"

"Because he was the enemy of my father, whose honour he calumniated, and whose fortune he endeavoured to overthrow. The man who was injured, nobly sought the defamer, fought with, conquered him! When I was a boy, I have often heard my father speak of him; and his name has always been hateful to me. Is he in the room?"

"No, he retired at ten; but I presume, Roncorone, your hatred does not extend to his ward?"

"Ah Alberti! is it possible that enmity can attach to such an object!"

"I will make her known to you then," said my friend; and leading me across the room, he introduced me to Rosolie Venzone.

I was soon convinced that her attractions were not confined to her person; her mind also was deserving of much admiration. I attached myself to her during the remainder of the evening; Alberti could not draw me from her; and when she left the assembly, my spirits decreased, and I became indifferent to the music and company.

Several days succeeded, and I saw not Rosolie: I looked for her most anxiously in every public place; but Alberti told me that she had not left her house since I met her, owing to a slight indisposition. How much did I regret that I could not present myself before her! I never could enter the doors of Salvini—never could endeavour to conciliate the affection of the traducer of my father's honour. At length, however, we met again;—I flew to her with rapture, and fancied that she regarded me with pleasure; there were no traces of her illness left; she was blooming, lovely!—Insensible to the beauty, wit, and elegance of every other woman, to ingratiate myself into her favour was my strenuous endeavour; and in my first attempts I happily succeeded, or flattered myself that I did. I joined neither in the dance nor the concert, but remained by the side of Rosolie, delighting my eye with her beauty, and my ear with her sentiments.

I wanted to speak to her of Salvini, but dared not to do it. Some little time afterwards, however, Alberti came, and whispered to me that Signor Salvini had just entered the room, and was coming towards Rosolie.—My friend led me away: desirous of seeing Salvini, I retired but a few paces, and standing behind a group of dancers, a seeming observer of them, frequently turned my eyes towards Rosolie, and anxiously watched for the appearance of her guardian. He afterwards came up to her, and placed himself on the seat that I had just vacated; I had never seen him before; and, seeing him now, my cheeks glowed, and my heart palpitated; for I was looking on a serpent whose sting had been impotently darted at my brave father.

Salvini *appeared* to me scarcely more than forty years of age; his figure was fine, his face handsome, and his eyes were of that nature which puzzles the observer in finding their true meaning;— they made me instantly suspect him to be deeply versed in the arts of hypocrisy. His attention to Rosolie was pointed; he did not leave

her for an hour; and then as he removed only to a small distance, I
ventured not to address her again during the evening. Salvini and
Rosolie retired early: Oh, how I envied him the pleasure of leading
her out of the room! and how great was my pain to think that *he*
was her guardian.

I went home soon after, and never enjoyed less sleep in one
night; Rosolie's image was productive of both pleasure and pain,
and I dreamt of her in my short slumbers. Oh my sweet one!—
About the hour of noon on the following day my friend Alberti
was introduced to me in my chamber; he bantered me concerning
my precipitate retreat on the preceding evening, and worked upon
me till he drew from me a full confession of my love for Rosolie.
But he laughed at my declaration, and ridiculed the solemnity
with which I had made it.

"Wherefore these looks of gravity?" he enquired; "and why
that stride of words and deep-toned accent?"

"Alberti, you are no lover."

"Roncorone, the ladies of Venice will tell you otherwise; and
those in Naples will corroborate the evidence."

"Which, united, will only convince me that you are a mere
gallant. My love is but in its infancy, or I could talk of it in——"

"In such terms as many other romantic fellows have done
before you. But I must leave you now, for I have an engagement at
one, and shall not be able to see you any more to-day. To-morrow,
at eleven in the forenoon, I will call on you; and I beg you will be
prepared to go with me to meet Rosolie."

"Where, where, my friend?"

"At Salvini's."

"Have I not told you, Alberti, that I despise Salvini—that his
sight is hateful to me—that my eye holds him in abhorrence?"

"True, young misanthrope: but you will not see Salvini in
Venice for the course of a month."

"Why? wherefore?"

"Because he this very morning set off for Vienna."

"Heavens! and Rosolie——"

"Is left by Salvini at his house: her only companion is Signora
Bianca, her guardian's maiden sister, whose optics are by no means
clear; whose ears are not very happy in catching any sound, except

such an one as is made by the discharge of a cannon; and whose heart, though it be that of an old maid, is so excellent, that I almost wish to creep into a corner of it. Adieu! Be ready on the morrow."

"I will! I will!" I replied with transport.

"At eleven, Roncorone."

"I shall not forget, Alberti."

"Farewel!" he said, taking me by the hand.

"Adieu, my dear friend!" I replied, returning his pressure.

"Roncorone!" said Alberti, returning.

"Signor!"

"Had you not better place the engagement in your tablet?"

"No, no! it is already placed in my heart!"

"How exquisite are the joys of the romantic!" cried Alberti, with a loud laugh, as he left the room.

The absence of Salvini filled me with transport;—for a few minutes I rejected the idea of entering clandestinely the house of my father's enemy; but the joy of meeting, seeing, and conversing with Rosolie, was exquisite indeed. I flattered myself that I was not an object of indifference to her;—and if, during the absence of Salvini, I could convince myself that I was actually loved by her, the best and sweetest hope that I had ever harboured would be realized. I thought nothing of fortune, of my own inability to support her with splendour, or of the rancour and enmity of Salvini;— there was in me much expectation of happiness, and little dread of misery; my mind was stored with those beautiful ideas which impart pleasure both to the soul and body of man; and I banished all those on which anxiety might have depended.—Fool! fool!

Alberti called on me the following day according to his appointment. My vivacious friend was always inclined to sport with what he called my philosophy; but I now seized him by the arm, and almost pushing him out of the house, entreated him to bring me before Rosolie as soon as possible.

In a little time we were at the door of Salvini, and almost immediately after introduced to Rosolie Venzone. As I drew near to her, I trembled, but it was with pleasure; my cheeks heated as I spoke to her, and my first words were not very distinct. Oh how lovely did she then appear to me! Signora Bianca was present, and Alberti made me known to her; but, owing to her deafness, she could not join in general conversation; my friend, however, attached himself to her, in order that I might speak more particularly to Rosolie. The sweetness of disposition, the good sense and beauty of Salvini's ward, were now more conspicuous than ever. When I first entered the room, I discovered a pensiveness hanging on her features; but the cloud soon went over, and her charms grew more splendid. What a heart, what a mind this woman possessed! She appeared neither more nor less than Nature designed her; her sensibilities were her own; and if she knew what affectation was, she had never practised it. I was solicitous of making myself appear deserving in her eyes, and consequently meditated an attack on her heart.

If these sentiments were somewhat romantic, the inspirer of them was not a common object. Our visit was long, and I was reluctant to depart. At length, however, it was necessary, and bowing to Signora Bianca, and wishing Rosolie good morning, we left the house. On the following day I repeated my visit, and, on the next after that, was also at Salvini's: scarcely a day elapsed now without my seeing my sweet Rosolie, and I very readily dispensed with the attendance of Alberti. Signora Bianca was always present when we met; she was mild, and not without understanding; her kindness to Rosolie made me respect her; she was entirely dependant on Salvini, and had not, I conjectured, ever heard that her brother and my father were enemies.

Salvini had been absent nearly a month, and had written from Vienna of his intention to return to Venice—a circumstance which I almost dreaded, fearing that it would preclude me from the society of Rosolie, to whom I had never directly spoken of my love;—but she must have seen it; such a declaration would, I feared, be thought premature: the anxiety, however, of knowing in what manner she would receive it, made me determine on making it before Salvini came back to Venice.

I had one morning the happiness of finding her alone; and my heart most sincerely, though secretly, thanked her for admitting me. Enquiring for Signora Bianca, I learned that she was employed in her closet; and as I knew her to be rigidly devout, I did not apprehend that, even if she were apprized of my being there, which was by no means probable, she would neglect her duties to come to me. The opportunity of declaring the state of my heart to Rosolie offered itself most favourably; I had often wished for it—often regretted that time and circumstances had never aided my design;—yet now both were auspicious; the object before me, smiling in her loveliness, and every thing agreeable to the purpose, I felt a concern, a restlessness, nay, even a timidity, and seemed almost to have forgotten the powers of language.

My abashment was that of unassuming and unaffected love: I was not, like many suitors of modern times, preparing a fiction for the ear of a fancied mistress, neither was I furnished with those phrases and sentiments which by others, conscious of their own disability, and barrenness of intellect, are kept in readiness, and fashioned without taste, without sensibility, and without discrimination. But I was going to speak on a subject which had alternately filled me with joy and sorrow, elevated and depressed me, raised me to hope, and sunk me in apprehension. The time was passing, and the opportunity going by. This reflection in some degree roused me; and I drew my chair nearer to her, and, in her eyes, found such sweet encouragement, that my heart was emboldened, and the spell of silence no longer on my tongue.

She was then throwing up the window, in order to bestow a small donation on a poor object in the street; I would not check the amiable impulse, but, when she again returned to her seat, took her hand, and enquired whether I had her permission to speak on a subject which related particularly to my happiness. It was at that moment the rosy blush came upon her cheek; a suspicion seemed to be passing over her mind; and after a short embarrassment and irresolution, she bowed her head to express her acquiescence.

"Dear Rosolie!" I exclaimed, "I thank you for this goodness. I say *dear* Rosolie, because I am prompted by my heart to do so; and because, in moments like these, I cannot attend to the cold construction of words and epithets."

"Signor!" said Rosolie, smiling—"Signor, pray what has this to do with your happiness?"

"Oh! much, much! I must now avail myself fully of your permission; and do not think me either inconsiderate or hasty, if, dispensing with those dull fashions and modes which spring from dull heads, or from frivolous hearts, I declare to you as sincere an affection, as ardent a love as ever rose in the breast of man, as ever was excited in the contemplation of loveliness and virtue!"

"Signor Roncorone, this declaration—"

"Is honest in all its principles: if uncourtly, it is true; if unembellished, its basis is sincerity. I repeat again, that I love you; and that you were dear to my eyes even at the moment they first beheld you."

"You confuse—you embarrass me——"

"Truth should never confuse; and virtue, like your's, dear Rosolie, can be but for a short period embarrassed by the humble declaration of an unassuming man, who fears he is not possessed of sufficient merit to raise in your mind, and to excite in your bosom sentiments and affections similar to his own. I fear all this; for he who modestly loves, must have many fears. To enter into any exordium on your person, sweet as it is to me, would have the tones of foppery; and to enumerate your virtues, and methodically comment on them, would place neither of us in a pleasant view; therefore, on these topics I would not enlarge, though it were impossible to remain wholly silent. In my hours of solitude, when my fancy raises your figure, then the corresponding qualities of your mind are also remembered; and then I can indulge myself in the reverie without being thought presumptuous. And yet, Rosolie, could I hope that there was a sympathy in your soul— could I hope for a return of affection——"

"Roncorone! I greatly esteem you."

"I thank you, Rosolie; it is a kind, a soothing, but not altogether a satisfactory word. You may esteem a thousand other men, though it might be difficult to say you *loved* so many. Oh that I were assured I was so happy a being as to be placed in the second class, and that those affections which I harbour for you were counterbalanced and equal in your bosom!"

"*And may they not be*, Roncorone?"

"And are they? *are they*, sweet Rosolie?"

"I never see virtue but I love it, as well as its possessor; and seeing it in you, I would have my respect increase, not diminish."

"Dear girl!" I exclaimed, "be more explicit. You lead me half way to joy, and I entreat you not to stop me in my course. Go on,

I conjure you; realise my hopes; and tell me that my wishes have not been repeated ineffectually."

Rosolie, smiling, but with a tear in each eye, was preparing to answer, when a servant came to her to say that Signora Bianca wished her to go immediately to her chamber. "Delay it," I cried, as soon as the servant had withdrawn, "delay it for a few moments, and leave me not unsatisfied."

"I cannot now stay," she replied; "we shall meet again."

"May I wait on you at this hour to-morrow?"

"Then, and at every other time, I shall be happy to see you."

"But may I, in the interim, be assured that you pardon my presumption?"

"There is no presumption on which I can place my pardon; no offence of which I can say, it is forgiven."

"But there is a *love* to which you *can say*, Be constant, and I will reward you!"

She took my hand as she was leaving the room; the tears, which had been rising in her eyes, dropped from them upon it, yet still she smiled with increasing loveliness, and filled me with rapture by exclaiming—"Be constant, and I will reward you!"

This was one of the happiest days of my life: I had never before tasted such felicity; my joy was observed by every person who saw my face, but from all I concealed the cause of my transports; my heart panted for the promised interview on the succeeding day, when I suggested I should be able to draw from Rosolie a still sweeter confession, and also to place before her those plans which love had so hastily and fondly sketched.—The next day, a little before the appointed hour, I set out for Salvini's house, which, though it were the mansion of my father's detested enemy, contained a treasure that I would not have exchanged for the wealth and grandeur of Persia.

My happiness was certainly tinctured with enthusiasm, for I was provoked to see any face, on this day, marked with anxiety; to every beggar I gave a piece of money, and observing one wretch more dejected than any other, I beckoned him into an alley, and doubling my donation, told him to be glad, and bless the name of Rosolie.

I found it necessary to sprinkle my imagination a little before I presented myself to her; and did not knock at the door until I found that my reason was more calm and governable. Being shewn into the room where I had, the preceding day, held the interesting conversation with Rosolie, while the servant went to inform her that I was there, I fancied that I heard a repetition of the sweet sounds which had then issued from her mouth. She did not immediately come to me.

She is diffident, I thought; she cannot keep the rosy blushes from her cheeks, and is ashamed of the suffusion; she trembles to meet her lover, and her timidity still remains to be conquered. Come, dear girl! come and be confident.—My eyes are for adoration, but not for rudeness; my speech would be simple, not bombastic; and if I seek for further goodness in you, I will entreat for it in the unaffected strains of love, and not dare to exact it either by loose insinuation, or by bold enquiries.

She came, just as my imagination had pictured her. Her eyes fell from my face to the floor; and her voice trembled as she spoke to me, though she endeavoured to appear composed. I tried to smile away her confusion, and also to remove it by speaking of the common topics at general meetings, and, for a while, forbore to allude to what had occurred on the day then last gone by.— This had the effect that I desired: she was again my unembarrassed friend; and our mutual reserve passing over, seemed to open the way for mutual love. Fortune befriended me in this interview as much as in that of the preceding day: no interruption was likely to be given to our conversation, as Signora Bianca, accompanied by a friendly devotee, was gone to matins.

"To admit you in her absence," said Rosolie, smiling, "would be by her, I fear, considered as an impropriety; but you had proposed calling this morning, and I had promised to see you: I was afraid, therefore, that a denial on my part would have sounded rather unfriendly."

"It would indeed," I replied; "I might, perhaps, have called it even cruel. Bianca, I believe, could not be so scrupulously delicate: besides, I have some reason to suppose that she has admitted me into her particular favour; for she always smiles good-naturedly when I approach her, and has several times given an oblique, and not unhandsome compliment, which made me more studious to increase the value of her opinion, and also to merit her friend-ship.—But, dear Rosolie, before she returns, allow me to renew the subject of yesterday—a subject which, for sweetness, exceeds every other that has met my ear from those prattling days when I listened to my beloved parent nurse, even to the moments in which I attended, with rapture, to your confessions!"

"Confessions! Roncorone——"

"Yes, my Rosolie! confessions.—Though you were sparing of your words, those which you did utter were kind evidences in my cause; and in your eyes I saw so much generosity, such a sweetly tempered regard, that all the doubts with which my mind was bur-thened, were shifted from it as the dark clouds are often driven from the sky of summer. But as in our nature there is an unappeas-able craving, and as the consciousness of being happy will often excite a wish to be happier still, may I—may I, dear Rosolie, hope that you will now confirm what you said yesterday, that you will—with delicacy I ask it of you—be less equivocal in telling the man to whom you are the first and best beloved object in the world, that—you love him!"

"I will! I will!" she cried; "our sentiments are kindred; hesita-tion would be insincere; concealment hypocrisy. I confess, and blush not to confess, that, before you had made to me any dec-laration, my heart had voluntarily given to you its best, its most ardent affections. This is, indeed, being ingenuous; but I am self-acquitted, and do not fear that you will condemn me."

"Condemn you!" I exclaimed; "condemn you! a thousand kind thanks to you, and as many blessings on you for your sincerity! And when I abuse it, may I become contemptible to the eyes of man, and sinful in those of God! It is now known to us—blessed knowledge!—that mutual love reigns in our breasts: mutual love has but one grand object, union; till that is effected, the sympa-thies, however nearly allied, cannot wholly comingle; in our plea-sures there is something yet to sigh for; and happy as we are, there are felicities still to attain.—Lovely as you now appear to me, and dearly as my heart at this moment prizes you, I hope a day will soon arrive when I shall fondly imagine that a brighter beam of beauty irradiates your face, and that your heart is enriched by many additional virtues!"

"Stay, stay, enthusiast!" cried Rosolie.

"Oh, check not my good and happy spirits," I replied, "nor banish my imagination from the banquet prepared by itself.—Allusions and insinuations are the practices of the weak and designing; of the former, when love is stronger than the understanding; of the latter, when villany is stronger than love; I therefore disclaim them for their unworthiness; he who admires sincerity, and I confess I do, will never willingly deviate from its ways. Circumstances, dear Rosolie, induce me to be brief—abrupt perhaps you will think me; yet allow me to ask whether I may not expect my love and assiduity to meet with an *early* reward—for a reward you have actually promised me; and whether, in the character of an husband, I may not strive to make myself still more worthy of your esteem, of your tenderness, and affection?"

"Oh no, Roncorone!"

"No! do not say so: you have confessed——"

"What I would again aver."

"That you are my friend—that you love no other man better?"

"None so well! I repeat it—none so truly!"

"God bless you for it! And what then should prevent our union? What barrier can there possibly be to such a circumstance?—Name it; I entreat you to name it."

"My poverty."

"Your poverty! your poverty!"

"Yes, that which chills many a noble heart—that which sends many a virtuous being to shiver in obscurity—that which curdles the milk of many a mother, whose breast is the only offering she has for her meagre babe—and that which once brought a thousand evils on my buried parent!"

She burst into tears: I begged her to be composed.

"I shall be, presently," she said; "I do not often yield to the weakness of complaint, and now will quiet it as soon as possible.— But as you may not be acquainted with my real situation, let me concisely inform you of it."

"It will distress you, dear Rosolie!—it will give you pain."

"No, not much; I am not entering into a narrative; a few simple words will be sufficient for my present purpose. My father, I grieve to say it, was a son of error; fatally attached to what are by many called the pleasures of life, and better known to the followers of dissipation than to the lovers and practisers of virtue. Yet he was not altogether destitute of good qualities; he however suffered them to stray from him too often, and was not solicitous enough to gain the general regard of the world; though many have spoken in his praise, and all who knew him, acknowledged the force of his wit and misapplied genius."

"He was not, I believe, a Venetian?"

"No, he was a native of Florence, and in that city he married my mother; a beautiful and accomplished woman, a branch of a considerable family, and endowed with a fortune superior to his own. The style in which, for several years, he continued to live, the magnificence of his table, the liberality of his soul, and his easiness to be imposed on, at length considerably impaired his fortune; but still anxious to court the opinion of the world, still loth to depart from his usual consequence, he went forward instead of retracting, and winked at the danger that seemed to be lurking near to him, when he should have prudently pondered on the means of preventing its closer approach.—About this time he lost his wife, my dear mother! It touched him; he mourned sincerely for her; resided a twelvemonth in retirement; and then—Oh what strange infatuation!—returned to Florence, to folly, to extravagance still more glaring and unbounded!"

"The fatal effects of an ill-regulated mind!"

"Ah! they were, indeed.—I was then young, and unconscious of his errors, as well as ignorant of his circumstances. The world smiled, and he was satisfied; the sycophants cringed, and he perceived not their duplicity; they commended, applauded, and he further strove to excite their smiles and admiration. At length, in the voyage of pleasure he met with a complete wreck;—the demands upon him were almost innumerable, and his fortune was not adequate to satisfy half of them. The whole of his property was wrested from him; and all those friends, those smiling friends, became as cold as the statues which adorned his vestibule, through which the hypocrites were accustomed to pass on their way to pleasure and luxuries. The reverse was dreadful to my father! Fearful of the malice of his creditors, he resolved to leave Florence immediately, and to retire with privacy to some place where he and his disasters should be unknown. I was sitting one evening with a female friend of my departed mother, who had, since her death, resided in the house, and took on her the duties of a governess, when my father rushed into the room, and having put a letter into the hands of my instructress, took me up in his arms, and carried me to a carriage that was waiting in the street. He sprang in after me, and we were driven away with such speed, that I began to express my childish fears, and enquire the cause of our unseasonable expedition; but taking me on his knee, and kissing me, he assured me there was no danger, and begged that I would not ask him any more questions of that nature. I obeyed him, and continued silent; but his sighs melted my heart, and when I laid my head upon his breast, I felt several tears fall from his eyes upon my face.

"We travelled all the night," continued Rosolie, "and rested but little on the following day. My young mind was impressed by the strangeness of my father's countenance, and he spoke to me in such mingled tones of tenderness and melancholy as I had never heard before. On the third day he declared he could go no further, and the driver was desired to stop at the first inn;—we were, however, at some considerable distance from an house of reception; and when at length we were driven to one, the strength of my father seemed to be wholly exhausted. He sent me to bed almost immediately, and soon after retired to his own; but when, in the morning, I ran to his chamber, I was told that he was very ill, and that a doctor had just been sent for. With my eyes full of tears, I undrew the curtains, and took hold of his hot hand;—raising himself with difficulty, he clasped me in his arms; but the Doctor then coming in, I was led from the room by one of the female servants of the inn. Going sorrowfully along a passage, some person spoke my name, and touched my shoulder, when, turning round, I perceived that it was Signor Salvini, whom I knew to be an intimate friend of my father. With great surprise he enquired who brought me thither. "My father, Signor," I replied, "my father!"

"And where is he?" demanded the Signor.

"Dying in that chamber!" I cried, pointing to the room in which he lay, and to which his friend immediately hastened.

"I promised," Rosolie rejoined, "to use but few words, and must not therefore be so minute in my description which, I confess, even now gives me great pain. The fever that had seized my father was too obstinate for the powers of medicine; I saw him only twice afterwards, and, in the last interview, with many, many struggles of affection, he gave me over to Signor Salvini, who was standing by the side of his bed, and bade me love and respect the man who had promised to be my protector, when the grave should have hidden from me for ever my last surviving parent. He died a few hours after having uttered this injunction!"

"Dear Rosolie!" I cried, "you are distressed, agitated!"——

"No, not much—not much; but the fatal errors of my father can never make me cease to love and pity him. Signor Salvini was travelling towards Venice when he met with us at the inn; and having buried his friend, and tenderly endeavoured to solace me, he took me with him the remainder of his journey, and I have continued to reside with him from that to the present period."

"Oh! that you had fallen under the care of some other man!" I cried.

"Why?" enquired Rosolie with quickness.

"It matters not now," said I, checking myself; "I only wish it had been my father to whom you had been consigned; that he and my mother had cherished and solaced you; and that their darling boy had grown up with you, and been the happy companion of your earlier days. Oh how I should have loved my sweet associate! You to speak of *poverty*, Rosolie! To plead it as a barrier to our union! Had you been rich, I might have loved you less; and you will remember that *I* am no Emperor. He who wisely searches for happiness, and has some knowledge of the best, and least precarious manner of obtaining it, will never consider a superfluity of wealth as the primary object.—Consent, consent, my Rosolie, to make the felicity of your Roncorone complete!"

"Roncorone's generosity," she replied, "deserves a greater reward than I can possibly bestow; but he shall ever find me a faithful and willing friend."

"Heaven bless you!" I exclaimed.—"Heaven bless you!"

My rapture almost overpowered me; I blessed her tongue for its assurances, and pressed her, trembling, to my happy bosom. Signora Bianca came into the room soon afterwards, and I thought she looked more earnestly at us than usual; she fixed her eyes on the blushing face of Rosolie, and did not speak to me with her accustomed good-nature. I addressed her several times; but she heard me somewhat coldly, and her manners were repulsive till I withdrew. I could not conjecture the actual cause of this behaviour; and knowing that she could not possibly have overheard us, I remained in suspense all the day.

On the following morning, however, I received a letter from Rosolie, which explained the mystery.—She addressed me thus:—

"Since I last saw you, Roncorone, Signora Bianca has been talking to me with great earnestness, and I have, in consequence of it, suffered much embarrassment and anxiety. Though her language seemed to me a little harsh, yet I believe she was prompted by the best of feelings and most friendly sentiments. She says that your visits have been too frequent; and that, having never been introduced to Signor Salvini, or spoken of by him, she fears she had acted incautiously in allowing your introduction to her and me by Signor Alberti. To her remarks she has added some insinuations; she tells me that she discovered confusion in my looks yesterday, and that your unusual animation originated from some particular cause; which cause she hinted at, and, at the same time, demanded of me what I could not calmly answer. You will not be admitted any more till the return of Signor Salvini, which, according to a letter that Bianca received this morning from Vienna, is delayed for another week. When he comes back to Venice, I trust that I shall see you again—that I shall be allowed to converse with, and assure you that you are still dear to the heart of

"ROSOLIE VENZONE."

The beginning of this letter filled me with sorrow and concern; but the conclusion inspired me with rapture. To be deprived of the happiness of seeing Rosolie was cruel;—to be loved by her, to be *dear to her heart* was, however, a joy that nothing could equal. At the return of Salvini she thought of our meeting again.—Salvini! was it likely that *he* would allow of my visits, sanction my love, or approve of my proposals?

Rosolie was a stranger to the affair between my father and her guardian: I had never told her of it; and as it had taken place at a great distance from Venice, and many years had since passed over, it was no longer spoken of, and known but to few. Entertaining the sentiments which I did for Salvini, could I possibly force myself upon his notice? Could I humble myself to, and solicit the man who had despised, reviled, and attempted to murder my noble-minded father? Impossible! So I first thought; but Rosolie being the object, I afterwards acknowledged that I could do any thing for her. My ill opinion of Salvini was merely hereditary; for I had seen little of him, heard little of his character; he was, however, reported by my friend Alberti to possess great pride and inflex-ibility, which he could occasionally very artfully cover; and my informer added, that he was a man of strong and violent passions. This intelligence certainly was not favourable to my designs; but thinking that it might probably be exaggerated, I was resolved to do any thing conciliatory for the obtaining of Rosolie.

I had not seen her for four days, when I contrived to have a letter conveyed privately to her, in which I conjured her to give me an interview of a few minutes. The bearer of my letter brought me an answer:—Rosalie was all tenderness; she named an hour when Signora Bianca would be with her Confessor, and appointed a place for our meeting at some little distance from the house. I could scarcely moderate my joy; I was at the spot of assignation almost an hour before that which had been appointed; my impa-tience was not to be restrained; and I foolishly thought the time lagged purposely to perplex me.

At length Rosolie appeared, and I caught her in my arms; she trembled greatly, tears were in her eyes, and she was apparently much distressed.

"I fear," she cried, "that I am acting with great impropriety; I am treating Signora Bianca with duplicity, and doing what might bring on me disgrace and opprobrium."

Pressing the flutterer to my heart—"Rely, beloved Rosolie!" I replied, "on the honour of your Roncorone. Our future meetings will not, I hope, be clandestine; and the world is too well acquainted with your virtues to attempt to sully them. Be composed; your agi-tation is distressing to me.—Oh how my heart thanks you for this kindness!"

I could not entirely quiet her apprehensions; and she urged me to be brief, as the time that Bianca's Confessor continued with her would probably not exceed half an hour. I led her to speak of Salvini, and she mentioned him in high terms, saying that he had been the steady friend of her father, and to herself very indulgent, kind, and even profuse; she confessed that to almost every other person he was exceedingly imperious and morose; but to her, and particularly of late, she added, he had shewn the most unbounded affection.

She spoke this with great simplicity.—I started—"Morose to almost every *other* person, and shewing to you *unbounded affection!*"

"Yes, Roncorone; those sentiments which he bore for my father, he has transferred to me."

This did not altogether quiet me; I however assumed a composure; and as I had urged for this meeting, partly to learn from her more fully the character of Salvini, and to inform her of all that I knew respecting him, which I had, for several reasons, hitherto neglected to do, I begged her to attend with patience to me for a few minutes.

"That my love for my sweet Rosolie is sincere as it is ardent," I said, "I think she will not question. If I am to go with her through life, happiness surely cannot be wanting; but should there not be such an union as my heart wishes for, to that heart must be attached an unfading regret, if not a ceaseless misery. Rosolie, how am I to attain you?"

"By declaring your sentiments to Signor Salvini on his return. I owe him much, and to make my union happy, I could wish to have his sanction."

"But what if he should withhold his consent? Will you give up Roncorone to despair and affliction?"

"No!" she replied, with great force.

"Not forsake—not abandon him?"

"Never! I have a sense of Salvini's favours and tenderness; I regard him as a father, and as such respect him;—to offend him might make me unhappy; but viewing him as I do, I cannot consider him as the arbiter of my affections, or as the director of my choice. My heart is your's, Roncorone. Salvini cannot force it into the possession of any other man."

Oh! what a confession was this! It made me almost extravagant. Relying on her promise, I now ventured to tell her of the affair that had formerly taken place between Salvini and my father; and also to hint my suspicions that he would, on that account, rancorously oppose our union. She started at the intelligence, and shewed many signs of surprise; but she soon gained her composure, and protested that whatever might be his opposition, she would ever adhere to the declarations which she had then made. She prepared to retire, fearing that Bianca would discover her absence; and, in order to avoid suspicion, she wished me not to accompany her home.

"Roncorone," she said, giving me her hand, "I have spoken as sincerity prompted me; but, believing you a man of honour, I fear not a failing in your discretion; I confide implicitly in you."

"Then you confide in one," I replied, "who values your person and happiness above every other thing on earth!"

She then left me to my joy, gazing on the beautiful visions of expectation, and listening to the ideal promises of hope. * * * * * * * My head seems as light as the down of the thistle. If a man of reason cannot be the guide of his own thoughts, how shall Roncorone, who is reputed mad?

* * * * * * *

Salvini returned to Venice: I was anxious to know the tenor of his sentiments as soon as possible; but Rosolie intimated to me that she wished me not to introduce myself immediately to her guardian. Her motives sprung from delicacy, and I attended to her injunctions, though they served to increase my impatience. Rosolie and I were unseen by each other for several days, and I spoke of my disappointment to Alberti, and also of my anxiety to convey to her a letter, without making it appear to the family in which she lived that she held a clandestine correspondence.

"Say no more, Roncorone," cried the gay Alberti; "at night you shall see the Madona of your idolatry; and I will undertake to convey any letter to her that you many please to write, and entrust to me. I was at Salvini's house about an hour ago, when I heard him tell the servants that he should be on the water to-night at eleven, and that Rosolie and Bianca would accompany him. I should know his gondola from a thousand others, if there were only half a beam of moon-light. What say you, Roncorone, to a revel on the waves of the Adriatic? Will you accompany me?"

I acceded to his proposal with true pleasure; wrote my letter; gave it to him;—and at ten o'clock went with him to the water. I knew not how he meant to deliver my epistle, but he told me to rely on his friendship and ingenuity. The paper that I had addressed to Rosolie, spoke of my recent mortifications and solicitude, and entreated her to allow me to introduce myself to Salvini without any further delay, in order that I might know whether he sanctioned or discountenanced my addresses.

Alberti knew at what place the gondola of Salvini was stationed; we therefore sailed but a little distance from it, and waited for the arrival of the expected party. At length Alberti told me he heard the Signor's voice; and directing my eyes to the spot that he pointed to, I saw Salvini assisting several ladies into the gondola. My ear caught the music of Rosolie's tongue; and the night was so clear, that I could plainly distinguish her figure in the group.

They rowed past us; Alberti did not discover himself, or give any salutation; I could scarcely refrain from speaking to Rosolie;— but my friend put his finger to his lips as a mark of silence, and followed them, though he kept at some distance. Salvini's party seemed in high spirits; but Rosolie seldom joined in the conversation, or, taking a part in it, spoke very faintly. I feared that she was depressed and unhappy; and the idea of her being so was sufficient to bring me to her imagined condition. We now drew nearer to the boat that contained her, when Alberti, having previously desired me to wrap myself up in my cloak, took a flute from his pocket, and played a solo with such skill and delicacy, that he instantly attracted the notice of every person in the gondola that preceded us.

Perceiving that he had drawn their attention towards him, he whispered me to step behind the curtain of a small silk canopy;— he then laid aside the instrument, and sung a canzonet in so superior and exquisite a manner, that he increased the interest he had at first excited.

"Alberti!" cried Salvini, recollecting the voice. The gondolas were now close to each other.

"Signor Salvini," cried Alberti gaily, "cannot you let a man shew his gallantry without bringing him into immediate notice? Had you suffered me to remain unknown, I would have played to you till I cramped my fingers, and sung you more songs than were ever written by Metastasio."

"Join our party," said Salvini, "and then you shall hear my apologies."

"I am sorry," replied Alberti, "that I am obliged to decline your invitation, having an engagement within an hour."

"But your song," said Rosolie, "has charmed me; and by singing it again, you will give me much pleasure."

Alberti sung again, and with increased effect; every person, except himself, was mute, when, peeping from behind the curtain, I saw the sweet face of Rosolie within a few yards of me. Alberti finished the air, and presented a paper to Rosolie.

"As you like the words," he said, "I will give you a copy of them; your smiles will sufficiently reward the poet. Here are copies also for your friends; distribute them, if you please. Signor Salvini, I have one left for you; the author is ingenious, but unfortunate; I have promised to solicit patronage for him, and will speak to you on the subject at some future time. Good night! pleasure attend you all!"

Ordering the gondoliers to take us on shore, we were separated from Salvini's party;—the presence of the men prevented me from speaking particularly to Alberti; and when we had left the water, he would allow me only a few minutes' conversation, during which he, however, told me that my letter had been delivered with the verses, and that it had not escaped the notice of Rosolie. He then broke from me, as it was near the time of his engagement, and left me to return home alone.

About noon on the following day I received a letter from Rosolie; affection never spoke sweeter words; and she allowed me to place myself before Salvini as soon as I pleased. When Heaven formed this woman, she surely was not destined for the lower world! She was—Ah! why should I torture myself by a repetition of her virtues and perfections?

I could not rest till I had spoken to Salvini; but, having to combat with a thousand apprehensions, I knew not in what manner to address him. My father rose in my mind, and contempt was forming for his enemy; conscious, however, that any expression or appearance of disgust would weaken my cause, I at length determined to bear myself with apparent respect, as I relied on the constancy of Rosolie, and hoped that Salvini would place no barrier between us.

Rosolie's letter had not reached me more than an hour when I availed myself of her permission, and hastened to her guardian's house. He was at home, and without any engagement;—having sent my name to him, and requested an interview, contrary to my fears, he readily granted it; and in a few minutes after entered the room into which I had been shewn.

"I entreat your permission, Signor," I said, "to address you as the guardian of Rosolie Venzone?"

"You have it," replied Salvini, without expressing much surprise.

"After this request, you will probably conjecture the cause of my now appearing before you?"

"Were I to do so," he answered, "I might be led into error; you will therefore please to explain it fully, Signor—Signor—"

"Roncorone is my name," said I, looking earnestly at him.

"True," cried Salvini, with a changing countenance, and with eyes scarcely able to shut up his indignation, "I would have you proceed, Signor Roncorone."

"I trust that a detail of circumstances is not necessary. I shall briefly say, that I have lately attached my heart and affections to Rosolie, your ward. I love her truly and ardently; to attain her would, I think, make me eternally happy; but to be kept ever apart from her would, I fear, be stripping life of all its choicest comforts."

I paused, but Salvini not speaking—

"Harbouring these sentiments," I continued, "and indulging those good hopes which are generally allied to our wishes, I now present myself before you, Signor, to entreat that you will countenance my affection, and also allow me intercourse and correspondence with Rosolie. I am informed that you have, for many years, stood in the place of, and acted as a parent to her; I consider myself, therefore, as now addressing you in that character, and hope that my present application will not be unsuccessful."

Salvini carried his eyes from my feet to my head, and I thought I saw contempt hanging on his lips; but the placid manner in which he afterwards spoke, led me to believe that my suspicions had done him injustice.

"Pray, Signor," he said, "is Rosolie acquainted with the nature of your sentiments?"

"I have made them known to her."

"And she approves them?"

"She has made me happy, very happy, in telling me so."

"And she has, I presume, referred you to me?"

"Yes, she gave me permission to speak to you on the subject."

"Signor Roncorone," said Salvini, "I have an engagement that prevents me from enlarging our conversation at this time.— Though I have been the protector of Rosolie, who, in her younger days, was consigned to me by her father, yet my power as a guardian is limited. Your acquaintance with her has been short; congenial dispositions, however, spurn at the reserve that custom has established, and soon open to each other. I have a sense of the honour done to me in being consulted, but can only say, that Rosolie must determine for herself; if you expect a more particular reply from me, you must first allow me to speak with the Signora. Call on me on Monday morning, and we will then, if you please, renew the subject."

He rose.—I bowed to him as I left the room, and was conducted to the door. Inclined to think that the sentiments of Salvini were in my favour, and that he regarded me not with malice for being the son of Roncorone, my hatred for him was softened;—and though I had said to Alberti that Salvini and I must never meet, yet Rosolie caused me to think myself not degraded by the advances which I had made to him. I was not then acquainted with the extent of the villain's hypocrisy.

Relying on the love and constancy of Rosolie, as well as on the approbation of Salvini, what expectations did I harbour! What beautiful prospects burst upon my imagination! Credulous, credulous Roncorone!

As Salvini had neither consented to, nor opposed my seeing

Rosolie, I knew not what to do in regard to going to her again; but as three days only had to elapse before I was to wait on her guardian, I endeavoured to content myself by writing to her an account of my recent interview. On the Monday I went to Salvini's house, and was soon brought before him; I bowed respectfully as I approached him; my sentiments were not so harsh as they had formerly been; and though I did not actually esteem him, yet I no longer hated him.

He did not receive me warmly, and the expression of his eyes was not understood by me: I thought, at one time, they glanced malignity; but the smile that immediately followed, again softened my suspicion. His face was often varying its colour; and though a calmness seemed to preside over his features, I could easily perceive that it was affected. I wished him to open the conversation; but finding him not inclined to do so, I began to speak of the object of my present visit, and he heard me with an unmoved countenance.

"Signor Roncorone," he said, "are you *sure* that the possession of Rosolie Venzone would make you permanently happy?"

"I hope—I trust it would," I replied warmly.

"She is not rich, Signor."

"I am not in search of fortune," I answered, somewhat hurt at his manner of speaking these words.

"Since I saw you last, Signor Roncorone, I have well considered your proposals and intentions; and having the happiness and *prosperity* of Rosolie at my heart, you must allow me to say that I cannot sanction your further addresses."

"Signor! do I understand? Did you not on Thursday give me flattering encouragement?"

"Encouragement! No; I only begged for time to think of the affair: I *have* thought of it, and repeat, Rosolie cannot be your's with my approbation."

"Astonishing! and the reason?"

"The incompetence of your fortune, and your want of rank."

"And have you no other motives?"

"None;—no other—these are sufficient."

"Recollect—do you now view me in my own character, or as the shadow of some one gone by? Is not your rejection guided by principles which have been long rooted, rather than by sentiments of a recent date?"

"You speak enigmas, Signor," said Salvini, with a reddened face.

"And if I do," I replied, "I will not put you to the unpleasant task of giving them solutions. You reject my proposals?"

"I do. As the object, therefore, is not to be obtained, I would advise you to root it immediately from your memory."

"Your advice is too unimportant for my acknowledgments; the object *is* to be, *shall* be obtained. Rosolie has a will of her own."

"And have I no influence as her guardian?"

"None sufficiently strong, I hope, to alter those principles which I know her to possess."

"But with the principles which she *does* possess," he said, "you probably are not well acquainted. I have conversed with her concerning you, and told her that my approbation would never attend her union with you."

"You *have?*"——

"I have. She listened to me patiently; and, by the manner in which she received my determination, I am led to believe that she can obliterate the slight impression you have made, without materially affecting her happiness."

"Signor Salvini," I exclaimed, almost swelling into passion, "you are speaking a direct and gross——No matter—you are deceived.—Rosolie loves me; and I am assured that she would not deny it to you.—The day of our union is not far distant, and I shall soon remove her from your house.—We thought it most respectful to apprize you of our intentions; but as you would unwarrantably impede them, I am happy that your power does not extend to your wishes."

Salvini seemed endeavouring to smother his flames:—"I told you at our first meeting," he cried, "that my power as a guardian was limited; but I now confess it is less so than you may imagine."

"You *can* then step aside from veracity? You confess it, worthy Signor Salvini!"

"Less irony, and more respect, if you please. I have a paper in my possession, given me by Venzone, the father of Rosolie, some few hours before his death, in which he enjoins her to submit herself to my direction, and, in the article of marriage, to rely implicitly on my guidance and approbation. If she spurn at these commands, I have yet to learn her character."

I saw through this shallow artifice, and looked on him as a contemptible liar!

"It is false!" I cried; "it is false! you have no such paper;—if you have, it is a recent forgery, a fabrication of a malevolent mind. Rosolie will discover the poor stratagem; and the sense of her obligations will lessen, when she discovers the inefficacious project."

"You talk insolently!" said Salvini, rising from his seat.

"Do I, Signor? Chastise me for it, if you dare. You know my opinion, nor will I retract. But be cautious how you treat me; if my passions are excited, they must be exercised; and should you, designedly, insult me, or obstinately place yourself as a barrier between me and happiness, you may probably, *a second time*, acknowledge your temerity *beneath the sword of a Roncorone.*"

The blood fled from the cheeks of Salvini, and he borrowed a look of the devil to throw at me. I instantly left his house, and went to my own, where, to my surprise, I found a letter from Rosolie; my eyes ran over the contents of it, which were of such an irritating nature, that my passion almost increased to madness, and my actions and exclamations nearly terrified my servant. She gave me an account of her interview with Salvini, repeated their conversation, and informed me that his motive for rejecting me was, in order that *he* might supplant me in her affections, and become himself her husband!—Oh, how I cursed the hypocrite!

She desired me to be patient for a few days; again assured me that her heart was wholly mine; that she contemned the trick of Salvini's forgery; and that, in the course of a week, she would quit his house, and give herself up to my love and honour. I resolved to comply with her request; but it was difficult for me to suppress my rage, and stifle the indignation that had been raised by the hypocritical dotard. His attachment to women was notorious, and his loose amours were generally known; but to think of making the blooming Rosolie his wife—the child of his friend—eighteen to fifty!—Contempt gave way to mirth, and my rage was dissipated by a hearty laugh.

Rosolie wrote to me again on the following day; and, by the

manner in which the letter was conveyed, I assured myself that Salvini had no knowledge of her correspondence with me. I found that he had once more been enforcing his passion, had offered to her half of his fortune, laid jewels before her, and vowed eternal love and tenderness!

"He also spoke of you," added Rosolie; "but in a manner which made me despise him; for he depreciated abilities which he cannot himself boast to possess, and strove to cloud those virtues which are superior to his nature. He has ordered his servants never to admit you again;—come, however, on Thursday morning, at the hour of ten; do not be repulsed; go immediately to his study, with which you are acquainted, and where you will probably find him. Tell him you are come to demand me of him;—but controul as much as possible your passions, and do not hint at the proposals which he has made to me. I shall be apprized of your arrival by a girl who attends me; I will come to you immediately, bid Salvini a last adieu, and shew you how much I confide in your affection and tenderness. The rigid and unimpassioned may censure us; but in retirement we will smile at their malice, and look for no approvers beyond ourselves. Roncorone, we have at present an assurance of happiness; and I trust that the time of its realization is at hand."——

Man is subject to such fine sensations as language can only coldly describe, and mine were of that nature. I hired a beautiful little retired house, and, in the course of four days, furnished it in a manner which I thought would please my Rosolie; I placed a man and woman servant in it, bought some music and instruments, and arranged the works of her favourite authors in the apartment intended for her use; my picture also was there, and I had fixed it in such a position, that it was sure to meet her eye on her first entrance. My * * * * *

* * * * * *

On Thursday morning, at the hour of ten, I entered the study of Salvini, having first silenced the insolent murmurs of the porter who opened the door, and pushed aside an interposing lacquey, who stood in the hall; and who doubtless acted according to the directions of his master. Salvini was not there, nor in any of the rooms below. Resolving to dispense with ceremony, I went up stairs, one of the servants following me, and looked into all the apartments, which were wholly deserted.

I was greatly disappointed, and the fellow who accompanied me, sneeringly asked whether I wished to extend my search; but desiring him to be less impertinent, and looking at him as if I would not be trifled with, he put aside his buffoonery, and informed me that his master, Signora Bianca, and Rosolie had left the city the preceding evening.—My vexation was extreme, and I could not conceal it from the attendant, of whom I impatiently enquired whither his master was gone; but the fellow protested he knew not, and also that he believed every other remaining servant was as ignorant in that respect as himself.

My passions almost choaked me; but feeling how much my distress pleased the low-minded menials of Salvini, and being assured that neither he nor Rosolie were in the house, I departed from thence with a sick heart, and an irritated brain.

I was divided between sorrow and rage, and a thousand conjectures crowded upon me; many of them extravagant and idle, others in the greatest degree tormenting, but some few of them, on being examined, appeared probable.

"The eyes of mine enemy have been vigilant, and his heart has been storing itself, even to fulness, with venom. I am hateful to him, because I am the son of Roncorone—because the noble-minded man from whom I sprang, chastised him for his lies and cowardice, and placed him in the notice of the world with all his villany on his brow.——He has been watchful over the actions of Rosolie, has employed emissaries; he intercepted her letter, in order to apprize himself of its contents; and, finding sufficient time for his envious projects, sent it to me to embitter the disappointment which he knew I must feel on finding her clandestinely removed from me."

"Dear Rosolie, I do, indeed, suffer as much as our malignant torturer could wish: yet, determined as he seems to place a thousand barriers between us, let me still hope that I shall remove them all, and in the moments of success and felicity, smile on the feebleness and impotence of his puny malice. The dotard loves her himself, and may have removed her merely to try the force of his eloquence; to plead a passion which nature refuses to aid, and to talk of love at an age when most good men are seriously preparing themselves for death.

"Though I am at present unacquainted with the place of Rosolie's concealment, I will be active in endeavouring to discover it; she will not long be hidden from me; we shall meet—we shall meet, and be happy, while the hated Salvini is writhing under the torments of a self-accusing conscience!"

So I murmured to myself as I walked along, endeavouring to subdue the passion that was then choking me, and to flatter myself that my difficulties would be soon and effectually surmounted. It was only necessary to learn the place of Salvini's retreat, to which, on procuring the information, I resolved instantly to follow, and rescue from him the beloved object, of which I had, some few hours previously to my disappointment, assured myself of attaining. In my attempt to be tranquil, I could not, however, wholly succeed;— I could not entirely quell the tempest of my mind, nor think of Salvini without cursing him for his treachery and hypocrisy.

I had not much to fear on Rosolie's account, being acquainted with the strength of her mind, as well as the extent of her affection; I knew that the arts of her guardian, as he mistermed himself, could neither impair her constancy, nor shake her fidelity; and that, though the precipitancy of his proceedings might, for a little while, alarm, they were not likely to seriously frighten her. It was some consolation to me that Bianca accompanied her; for I had long since discovered that the old lady's heart was most tenderly attached to her, and that her love was little short of the maternal.

There was yet no stability in my mind;—if, for a moment, I listened to the voice of hope, in the next, vexations crowded upon me so fast, that patience was beginning to quit me. In this state I sought my friend and usual adviser, Alberti, to whom I was indebted for making me known to my dear Rosolie, and also for assisting me in my secret correspondence with her. I hastened to his house, in order to inform him of my disappointment, and to entreat his advice and assistance; but my perplexity increased by not finding him at home, and it was late in the following morning before I could obtain an interview with him.

On seeing him I hastily recounted the occurrences of the preceding day, and stated the views I had had respecting Rosolie, the abrupt departure of Salvini from Venice, and the provoking overthrow of the project which I had so fondly thought would bring me a large store of happiness for future years. Alberti was at first inclined to laugh at my gravity; but seeing my real uneasiness, his friendly heart instantly admitted sympathy, and no longer indulged itself with mirth.—The admirer of human beauty must at all times have been pleased with the face of Alberti; the transition of his features gave to the imagination the picture of a spirit, who either smiles or weeps, and whose variations of countenance succeed as rapidly as the clouds amid which it sails on its white downy pinions.

"Dear Roncorone!" he exclaimed, with tenderness, "excuse the levity of my nature, for which I often have to blush; still it is always in your power to give gravity to my substance, and there is not another man on earth than yourself, in whose concerns I would so willingly engage, and whose joys and sorrows I would so readily make my own."

"I thank you, my good friend," I replied, "but I have lost Rosolie!"

"She is again to be found."

"But how? Tell me how?"

"Certainly not by despondency and complaints, but by activity and enquiries."

"The servants of Salvini are obstinate, and not to be bought; I have not had time to seek elsewhere, nor do I know where to apply for information. My disappointment has almost staggered my reason; and I can scarcely act consistently. You, Alberti, must assist me; you must endeavour to procure that information for which my soul is craving; you must aid me in discovering the place of my Rosolie's concealment, and exert yourself in promoting our union."

"I will proceed in my deputation immediately," replied Alberti; "and I think I may venture to bid you rely on the success of it. Salvini has a wide circle of friends in Venice, and it shall be my business to worm them all, if it be possible. To lock up our projects within our own breasts, and communicate them to no one person, is more often pretended than performed. Salvini has doubtless opened to some acquaintance; and though he probably subjoined an injunction of secrecy, yet I know that secrecy is but an irritating nettle; and if I only meet with the man who is so entrusted, my life on it that I extract from him the mystery."

"I thank you, I thank you, most fervently," I replied.

"Stay till I shall have done something to merit your thanks, Roncorone; animate yourself! The stolen jewel shall be returned, beaming with a thousand additional hues and lustres."

"You are an excellent comforter, Alberti! But have you no conjecture where the retreat of my opposer may be?"

"I know of no established residence that he has, except in this city; some time since he disposed of his estate at Ferrara; besides, if privacy be his motive, as it appears to be, he has certainly chosen some remote and less frequented spot for his abode. He has transactions of some nature in Germany, which country he has visited several times within the last four years."

"And thither he has probably conveyed my Rosolie?"

"It may be so, indeed."

"I will go after her—I will pursue her—I'll bring her back from thence."

"Travel not so far," said Alberti, "by the vague directions of conjecture; for, should your route commence with error, you might not be able to surmount the difficulties which would be attendant on it. Much as I love an ardent spirit, I would not be regardless of the voice of caution. Be patient for a little while: I will go out now, and make some few enquiries; should I procure any information, I shall almost, on the instant, be with you; and in the evening, whether successful or disappointed, you may expect to see me. Adieu, dear Roncorone!"

He left me; and I hoped, when I next saw him, to hail him as the messenger of happy intelligence; I knew his activity of mind and body, his winning address, and easy manner of ingratiating himself into the affections of all those who listened to him; and from these qualifications and accomplishments I augured much that was good and favourable to the cause. Endeavouring to rouse myself from the despondency that had been gathering around me, I went on the same pursuit as my confidential friend; but as I knew

not so many of Salvini's acquaintance as Alberti did, I hoped my
ill success would be compensated by a store of happy intelligence
from him within a few hours.

All, on my part, ended in disappointment; my exertions entirely
failed of success; and I could not discover even a slender clue to
lead to the information for which I was so anxiously seeking. My
passions were again becoming turbulent; the name of my malignant enemy *would* gather a curse as it came from my mouth; and
thought after thought ran tormentingly after my faithful Rosolie. I
was continually watching from the balcony, as long as it was light,
for the return of Alberti; but he did not appear before me till ten
o'clock, and then the coldness of his countenance chilled me.

"What news? what news?" I hastily enquired; "have you succeeded, or failed in learning the route of Salvini?"

"I must confess," he replied, "that I have been unsuccessful."

"Unsuccessful! and made *no* discovery?"

"None of importance, though I have been employed ever since
I left you, and very actively too."

"Alberti," I cried, "the treachery of my enemy will make me
mad. My poor Rosolie! how acute her sufferings must be!—Could
you learn nothing from the servants of Salvini?"

"I really believe," replied my friend, "that they know not what
journey their master has undertaken; if they are acquainted with
it, I could not persuade them to divulge it, though I offered the
contents of my purse to every one of them on that condition, and
also spoke to them in the mildest terms of persuasion."

"And they continued silent to this?"

"Obstinate as mules in an unfrequented tract.—'They knew
not—they could not tell; the Signor had not thought proper to
inform them. This was the general jargon from my first enquiry
to the last.'—The gravity and perverseness of the rogues vexed
me; and from them I ran to the different houses where Salvini
had acquaintances. There again I was disappointed: I prefaced my
enquiries to the men with politics, and those to the women with
flashes and antics of unmeaning gallantry: I succeeded in getting
them all into good humour; but when I asked the question which
induced me to make the visits to them, I only heard, 'Is the Signor

from Venice?—You surprise me—indeed I know nothing about him.'

"I assure you, Roncorone, I have had a tedious day of it: one old lady clacked in my ears incessantly full two hours; and the Marchesa di Castello fixed me in a corner of her music-room to hear her shriek out a score of new airs most infernally unharmonious.—I am sorry, very sorry that your ambassador should return to you with such indifferent success."

"Good Heaven!" I exclaimed; "what is to be done? What would you recommend, Alberti?"

"Patience: in the course of a few days we may be able to make the discovery."

"But, in the meantime," I cried, "my beloved Rosolie may be exposed to the impertinence of the odious Salvini's passion."

"What!" exclaimed Alberti, smiling;—"his passion? No, no, that is too ridiculous."

"But it is true," I replied; "he has professed to her his love, absurd as it may seem to you; and the man who can call the sunshine of benevolence upon his face, and at the same time be filling his heart with rancour, is capable of every thing that is degrading, base, and vicious."

It was late when Alberti left me; but previous to his departure, he strove to raise my spirits, and to——

But pause, Roncorone.—A pain seizes thy head, and a sickness comes over thy heart. God knows how long thine eyeballs will collect the light which his mysterious hand shoots over the immensity of space.

* * * * * *

I endeavour to observe the rules of method and unity in my narrative; but if my outlines are broken, kind stranger, whoever you are, remember that I am little better than a distracted man; often witless as the ensnared bird, and sometimes wild as the mountain torrent that draws dull and sullen echoes incessantly from my shapeless cavern. God! God! how strange do I appear when self-examined!—Am I on earth? Have I substance? Do I breathe? or, has the world of shadows received me? Am I wandering a spirit of misery? Am I suffering purgatory for vices and impurities into which I ran, contrary to the monitions of the supreme Father of the Heavens? These are frequently my questions: but, at this time, I have no doubts; let me therefore avail myself of the present tranquil moments, and proceed.

When Alberti left me, I retired to my chamber; but sleep and I were at variance, and I took no repose from midnight to the dawn of day, when I rose from the bed on which I had carelessly thrown myself, and let some air into my chamber to refresh me.—The infamous conduct of Salvini astonished and disgusted me the more I thought of it; there was such a poverty in his resentment, and such a meanness in his malice, that I could but regard him as a sorry and venomous reptile, deserving to be crushed under my feet. His clandestine departure, and the privacy observed respecting it, reduced him to a still meaner object, and plainly shewed that he feared the anger which he knew he must excite within my breast.

The recollection of my prospect on the preceding morning, when I went forth to claim my dear Rosolie, only served to make this more gloomy and disgusting: the fabric of hope was shaken; my expected joys, for the present, were driven far beyond my reach, and I knew no means of speedily bringing them within it again. I had no fear of either time or distance subverting the affections of Rosolie; but believed that there was a mutual stability in our loves, and that the one was no more capable of change or of duplicity than the other.

The joint enquiries of myself and my friend Alberti were as unsuccessful this day as they had been on the preceding; nothing was to be discovered, nor did any circumstance favour us in our search; the artful Salvini had well-regulated his plan, had used great caution in his retreat, and apparently had not entrusted the nature and cause of it to any second person. I endeavoured to quell my rage, and also to subdue my sorrow; and Alberti strove to console me by observing, that forerunning disappointments made the attainment of our wishes infinitely more precious.

"Were I situated as you are," my friend would say, "I would not bend my brows at what you call disappointments, particularly if, like you, I were assured of the constancy of my mistress's heart, and the strength of her mind, and that I believed neither of them would fail beneath the petty tyrannies and artifices of her guardian. I should look on my prospect as on a distant rainbow, viewed from an eminence on which the clouds were still lowering, and should trust that a tranquillity would succeed my disasters, even as the richer colours are diffused from the partial spot gradually over the whole horizon. Take my opinions, dear Roncorone; make them your own; and do not peevishly quarrel with Happiness, because she has left you for a little while to bid good-day to some other fellow of the earth."

Thus he talked; I listened, and for a short time thought it reasonable, and that my discontent and anxiety had not a sufficiency of cause to rest upon; but when a week had paused over since the departure of Rosolie, and several days of another followed it, I could listen no longer to such offered consolations, neither could I restrain the rage, nor quiet the grief that alternately swelled and agonized my breast. The inactivity in which I had remained, was in some moments a reproach to me; and I sometimes formed the extravagant notion of quitting Venice, and beginning a random search; but when the confusion of my intellects subsided a little, I plainly perceived the absurdity of such an expedition, which no person, possessing any degree of reason, would think of undertaking.

I wonder that the frequent irritations of my mind did not almost reduce me to a state of insanity. Nature had not formed me of torpid matter, but had given to my constitution a large portion of fervour, by which my passions were too often actuated; and my perplexities, and pangs of wounded affection, were nearly formidable enough to destroy the springs of my intellects. Although the enquiries of Alberti remained wholly unanswered, and his best expectations had been entirely baffled, yet he neglected none of the offices of friendship, but, on the contrary, was more studious in displaying them. The disease of my mind was not much amended by his solicitude (for which, however, I was grateful to him); and his endeavours to assure, comfort, and amuse me, generally were unproductive of benefit.

He had one morning, about a month after the departure of Salvini, been talking with me a considerable time, and was rising to depart, when my servant came into the room, and put a letter into my hand. I looked at the direction—Heavens! the pleasures of that moment will never be forgotten. I ran up to Alberti, threw my trembling arms around his neck, and burst into tears of joy.

"She is found!" I exclaimed, "she is found! Here is intelligence of my Rosolie; and it comes from her own hand. Oh dear Alberti! she is found, and by her am I summoned to happiness!"

"Read it, read it!" cried my participating friend.

I sunk into a chair, broke the seal, and hastily threw my eyes upon the lines; but an obscurity was placed before them, which, for several moments, prevented me from deciphering a single sentence; and I could not distinguish any of the characters of the letter. When I was a little recovered, I did not scruple to let Alberti know all that it contained; he was a sincere, generous friend, an almost brother, and had taken such an interest in my concerns, as entitled him to an unequivocal confidence.

I read the letter to him. Crazed as my brain has since been, I believe my memory still retains it. In the moments of my saddest affliction, I repeat many passages of it over and over again, and they melt me to childishness, and make me as tender as the little ones of the herdsmen, who stroll into the valley to gather the uncultivated flowers to braid into wreaths for the necks of their favourite kids.—Thus my Rosolie wrote:—

"My hand trembles, my heart is swelling in my bosom! My dear friend! my Roncorone! Oh, I cannot write that name without shedding many tears; but they are accompanied with a sensation which I wish not to stifle. These are my first happy moments since I saw you last, at least since Signor Salvini carried me from Venice to this place; from that hour till the present I have been prevented from writing to you; and no person would listen to me when I spoke your name, except Signora Bianca, whose brother has treated me so unjustly; and even she, poor pensioner on kindred authority! entreated me to desist, though she did it with gentleness.

"Oh! how I thought of you on the day I had named to quit the protection of my guardian, for that which you so tenderly offered me. I fancied that I saw you in an hundred different situations—astonished, disappointed, confounded. Salvini then appeared to me a most odious creature, and I had not a single good sentiment to bestow on him. Dear Roncorone! let me endeavour to account for my disappearance; but indeed anxiety has so preyed upon my mind, that, for several days past, I have felt a giddiness which has almost deprived me of my senses."

"On the morning preceding the day I expected to accompany you to your home, I was in my chamber, arranging some trifles for the morrow, and happily thinking of you, whom I considered as my best and most generous friend. My heart was gay; confidence attended my affection; and in the mirror of my mind I saw you as a dear and worthy object of honourable love, deserving of every thing the poor Rosolie could render you back, and of infinitely more than she had means to bestow. Thus harmonized, and my little concerns adjusted, I sat down near the window, when the door of my apartment was opened, and my surprise greatly excited by the appearance of Signor Salvini, whom I had never been accustomed to see in that part of the house. A foreboding of evil came across my mind: I raised my eyes, and, as he approached me, looked in his face, over which was spread a sarcastic smile, more alarming to me than the frowns and contractions of anger would have been.

"He came close to me, seated himself by my side, and took a paper from his pocket, which he unfolded and perused, but in a manner that then led me to suppose he had previously acquainted himself with the contents of it.

'Perhaps,' he said, withdrawing his eyes from what he had been reading, 'perhaps my present visit may be deemed an intrusion; this is, I confess, a place to which I have not been accustomed to follow you;—but had you been less solicitous to seclude yourself, there would have been no occasion for me to disregard the general rules.'

'Signor,' I replied, 'there have been times when to me you did not think any thing like an apology necessary; the daughter of Venzone has not, till of late, been accustomed to such ceremony. But if you please, I will withdraw into another room.'

'With your pleasure,' he cried, 'I will remain here; the conversation I wish to hold with you may soon be gone through with;—be pleased only to inform me what you know respecting this letter.'

"He put a paper into my hand, and with confusion I saw that it was a copy of the letter that I had sent to you, my dear Roncorone. I read it through, endeavoured to collect myself, and feeling the glow of resentment in my breast, enquired by what means he had become the possessor of the original.

'By suspecting,' he replied, 'that you were acting unworthily; and by exercising a privilege which caution hinted to me I was entitled to.'

'What!' I exclaimed, 'by intercepting my letter; by breaking the seal, and *stealing* the intelligence it contained?'

'I confess, my gentle ward,' he answered sneeringly, 'that your conjectures fall exactly upon the case, and that the means you mention were actually those which I employed.'

'There was not much honour in the action,' I said, roused, for the first time, to speak to him with acrimony; 'it has, in my eyes, made you appear a new character, and less deserving of the respect which I have ever been studious to pay to you.'

'You are very unequivocal,' said Salvini, with a varying colour; 'I did not expect from you so open an avowal.'

'Whatever I do,' I replied, 'I can ever avow; and whatever I think, I dare generally reveal. I should be lessened in my own estimation if I were to disacknowledge what you have charged me with. I wrote the letter to Roncorone, and it is expressive of my true sentiments; I love him, wish to be united to him, and to-morrow, as I proposed, I shall give you my last thanks, and seek for happiness with the man whose wishes you would oppose.'

"Salvini drew still closer to me.

'You are deceiving yourself!' he cried; 'you shall not even see him to-morrow; if I can prevent it, you shall never see him again. Marry Roncorone! my most determined enemy! I would rather give you to the jaws of a crocodile, a monster which is not more cruel or deceitful. Mine you *will* not be; his you never *shall* be!'

'Hear me, Signor Salvini,' I cried.

'I will hear you no longer, ungrateful girl! I shall leave Venice within a few hours; my sister goes with me, and you shall accompany us. I would seek for the remotest spot on earth to place you in, rather than yield you up to Roncorone. Prepare yourself, therefore, for the journey, for I am resolute; and if I cannot be loved, I will be obeyed.'

"He then rose. I strove to detain, and to speak further to him; but he put me down on a seat, and snatching up some pens and paper that were lying on the table, he hastily left the room, and locked me up in it.

"I wished to be resolute," continued Rosolie, "and to brave his malice; but, dear Roncorone, I thought of you, and tenderness immediately filled my heart; astonishment overpowered me; I could not banish the weakness I contemned; and sinking nearly into a state of insensibility, so I remained a considerable time, and till the Signor came to summon me for the journey. Starting up, I declared I would not accompany him; but he took me in his arms, and, being very powerful, carried me down stairs, and through the garden, and put me in a gondola, by the side of poor Bianca; he immediately sprang into it himself, and, by his directions, we were rowed from the shore. I placed myself still closer to Bianca, who threw one of her arms around my neck; I knew it were impossible to make her hear me without speaking very loud, and therefore did not attempt it; but I felt the tears of the affectionate woman drop on my hand, and could hear her striving to suppress her sobs, which she seemed to fear would reach the ears of her brother.

"Salvini remained silent a considerable time, keeping at some distance from me; at length he drew nearer, and offered me some refreshments, but I refused them with a motion of my head only, for I could not speak while my heart was so burthened. In about two hours we were set on the shore nearest to the city; and I found that Salvini had not neglected his arrangements, for a carriage was waiting for us, and in it we travelled two days before we reached this place, which I found had not been in any manner prepared for our reception. Here have I, since that time, resided a prisoner, with neither books to read, nor writing materials to make use of, only in this one instance; hearing every hour new insults heaped upon you, and also declarations of love from a man who is older even than my father would have been, had he been now living.

"Oh Roncorone! how many times has my heart been springing towards you!—How many times in an hour have I thought of you, and how many tears have been shed by me since our separation!

Salvini has seen my sorrow, and smiled at it; to have my weakness reviled and ridiculed, has, in some degree, inspirited me; and when my oppressor is present, I endeavour to wear the mask of indifference, though, in my bosom, I am actually carrying an almost broken heart. Is this our felicity, my dear Roncorone? No, no—let us hope it is yet to come! Poor Bianca is considerably indisposed, and in her I have lost a tender friend; lost, I say, because she is confined to her chamber, and her haughty brother so far resents my conduct, as to forbid my attending her. What a reverse of manners and sentiments in this man! He is now shewing himself to me as a character of which I had no conception, and leading me to believe that there is a species of hypocrisy which can a long time, even for a series of years, escape the eye of vigilance itself.

"Dear Roncorone, hasten to me, and snatch me from the lure into which I have been incautiously betrayed;—in your protection I shall be secure; these insults will then no longer reach me, and my enemies will have a chastiser. Hasten, dear Roncorone, and release me from this unwarrantable detention. Resolved to resent the tyranny of Salvini, I seclude myself as much as possible, accept none of his invitations, and seldom converse with him. Proud, stubborn, romantic—such are the terms he fixes to my conduct; and the epithet of ingrate has not been forgotten, but cruelly subjoined to them.

"We are living in a most retired spot, and I was a stranger to its name till within a few days, when I learnt it by hearing, from my window, the enquiries of a traveller, directed to one of the peasants of the village, and also the answers of the latter. It is a small habitation, nearly environed by mountains.—Bianca told me she had never seen it before, but had been informed that it became the property of her brother by the bequest of a relation, who has been some considerable time dead. After thinking of you, my dear friend, all the day, how melancholy it is to view on the eminences the last person that evening will allow me to observe! My eye follows him from the lower to the higher hill; I see him lessening with regret; and when he either winds from my sight, or is lost in the twilight obscurity, my heart will grow still more sad, its oppressions heavier, and spreading my hands on my disturbed bosom, I exclaim—'Oh that yon traveller were Roncorone, coming to remove the sorrows of his Rosolie!'

"I have been denied the use of a pen by Salvini, and I now write to you by stratagem. One of the domestics of the Signor is a benevolent and humane creature; I have given him money for his family, promised him a larger donation, and he has, contrary to the absolute commands of his master, not only furnished me with the means of writing, but likewise assured me that he would convey this letter to you. Good fellow! my Roncorone shall be your friend for this!—I am loath to break off, though my paper is nearly filled, and I have used the smallest characters in it. Come to me, Francesco, as early as possible; I shall not fail to look every hour in the day for you from my window.—Restrain your rage on seeing Salvini. There is a species of beings whose unworthiness is better regarded with a silent contempt than with angry invectives; such is Salvini, and *as such* I would have you regard him. God bless you! God bless you! Oh how happy will be that moment when my tongue shall convey such sounds to your ears; the idea of our meeting gives a thrilling pleasure to my heart. Adieu, best beloved, and most deserving friend of

"ROSOLIE."

These were the words that I read to Alberti, and with emotions nearly similar to those which a parent may be supposed to feel, whose eye feasts on an account of the prosperity of a favourite child, who had been long considered as sleeping in the earth of a distant country, or as lying a skeleton in the secret caverns of the ocean.

"Alberti!" I cried, pressing him in my arms, "Alberti! this is one of the most joyous moments of my life! I now perceive both the folly of despondency, and the comforts of anticipating good. I am re-animated; a new spirit has been infused into me—it is in every vein; it hangs on every fibre; it has entered each recess of my new moulded heart;—smile with me on my happiness! No gravity to-day; for to-day, within the present hour, I shall seek my sweet Rosolie!"

Alberti did not immediately speak, but he looked very strangely at me.

"*Where* will you seek her, Roncorone?" he afterwards enquired.

"*Where!* How singular is that question!"

"I must observe," he continued, "that the letter either does not contain such information as is necessary, or that I did not hear you read it. Peruse the paper again, and see if you can discover the clue, without which every thing must return to its former obscurity."

I carried my eyes over the letter again.—His remark staggered me—I found not any proper direction. I once more examined it; his observation was just; and, almost frantic, I exclaimed, "There is no direction! there is no particular mention of the place of her residence! This new disappointment will nearly bring distraction on me!"

"It is indeed most unfortunate," said Alberti.

"Oh, it is insufferably severe!" I cried, sinking in a chair; "it is too much for my heart—too much for my brain. This letter had given birth to a thousand new and delightful hopes; it has now sent into my mind a thousand apprehensions, and filled my breast with as many pains. The forgetfulness of Rosolie is astonishing; and it must necessarily bring sorrow to her, as well as to me."

"She has not been forgetful," said Alberti; "allow me to look at the letter.—She has *not* been forgetful—I see through it all. There are new stratagems on foot, Roncorone; deceits are practising on you, and villany is again directed towards you by your most inveterate enemy."

"What do you mean, Alberti? For Heaven's sake, tell me what you mean!"

"I will state my opinion, Roncorone, on this subject, because I believe it to be just.—My conjecture is, that the servant in whom Rosolie confided, is a rascal of hypocrisy and deceit; and that, aiming at two rewards, he having received one of them with the letter, from the person who wrote it, on the assurance of conveying it to you, afterwards sought for the other by delivering the packet with which he had been entrusted, and by divulging, with a feigned appearance of fidelity, all that he knew relating to it to Salvini."

"Speak on," I cried; "speak on!—Oh! I am growing wild with rage!"

"I shall say no more," replied my friend, "if you will thus suffer yourself to be disturbed by my conjectures."

"I will be tranquil, dear Alberti; pray proceed."

"My suspicion also leads to these points: that Salvini opened and read the letter; and that, in order to wreak his vengeance on you, to make your sufferings as acute as possible, and to be further revenged on Rosolie for her rejection, he removed the name of the place of her residence from the letter; and also, satisfied that it could not otherwise be known to you, in the moments of his triumph forwarded the composition, by which he assured himself of increasing your pain and concern."

"I do believe, Alberti, that you have fathomed his villany."

"No, that were impossible. But I have, I think, sounded it pretty deeply. One circumstance serves almost to verify my suspicions: look at the corner of the letter—it is torn; there had Rosolie written the name of the place in which she is confined; and Salvini had no difficulty in removing it without giving the paper a mutilated appearance, or destroying any of its essential characters."

"It is plain—it is evident—I see it all.—You have shewn the villain to me as he actually is, designing, malicious, and cruel. As to the minor rascal, he has fashioned himself by observations on the conduct of his employer; and may Heaven refuse me mercy, if I do not punish both of them according to the different degrees of their perfidy and baseness!"

"Rush not into the extremes of passion," said my friend; "be patient."

"Patient! If the vessels of my body were emptying, I could not be patient on such an occasion as this. Oh Alberti! existence never before laboured under such a complication of evils. My heart is sick with grief, and my brain hot with rage. To take with these hands the life of Salvini, I should scarcely consider as a deed against the laws of Nature; for can the assassin be hardly more deserving of death, than the man that privately tortures the soul, and racks the imagination of a fellow-creature, who never did any thing to deserve his enmity? The wheel has had victims not half so culpable, and gibbets have suspended carcases of wretches, who, in life, were more virtuous, and in actions more honourable than Salvini. My Rosolie, too——"

I threw myself into the arms of Alberti;—and if there be folly in the tears of a man, still I confess I wept. I could listen to no consolations, for I had been too often deceived; and therefore entreated my friend to offer me none.

"Can I," I cried, "be in any degree happy or composed, when I know my Rosolie to be the captive of Salvini, and even the sport of his menials? At this moment she may be suffering under their united cruelties and insults; at this moment subject to the fulsome love of her autumnal lover—curses on the dotard! or, freed a while from his detestable company, perhaps her eyes even now are wandering with fond expectation over the mountains, to greet the approaches of him who knows not in what spot to seek her."

"We shall, I trust, discover it soon, Roncorone."

"Pray, Alberti, nurse not my sick imagination with hopes; had I been less willing to believe, I had been less unhappy. Good Heaven! how shall I conduct myself? How repel the attacks which are made upon my reason? If my anxiety be not soon removed, and if the discovery of Rosolie be long protracted, I fear a total failure of that vigour and power which should accompany the chastisement of her infamous detainer."

I called my servant, and made some enquiries respecting the letter; but learning from him only that it came in the usual manner, I turned dejectedly from him to Alberti, who continued with me the remainder of the day, striving, but in vain, to lessen my concern and unhappiness.

The next ten days went over, during which, neither I nor Alberti were able to trace Salvini even a single mile;—we again went among his acquaintances, again applied to his servants; it was not, however, to any purpose that we did so, for our efforts in every quarter were repulsed. All of them wondered where Salvini was; but none of them knew, or would acknowledge it. Many wished to be informed why I so often enquired concerning it, and others insinuated that my motives were not hidden from them. Sick, feverish, and disgusted, I kept myself more at home, well knowing that Alberti would be active in my behalf; and at the end of another week a second letter from Rosolie was put into my hands.

I uttered an exclamation of joy when I received it; but, fearing to discover a stratagem similar to the one that had been before practised, my heart almost immediately sunk, and I unfolded the paper with considerable agitation. The shape of the paper was perfect—it was perfect!—that gave me a momentary pleasure; but the rapid idea of her thinking it unnecessary to name the place a second time, again nipped the expanding bud of hope. This was her letter; I repeat it from memory only:—

"What can possibly occasion your absence, Roncorone, since I have apprized you of the place of my residence, and told you, that to see you was my most anxious wish? When I last wrote to you, what a scheme of happiness did I form! The injuries I had received were almost buried in the hope of our meeting; I nearly forgot my confinement, noticed not the sarcasms of Salvini, and scarcely thought myself unfortunate.—Circumstances, I would say, in privacy, have been rather unpleasant; Salvini has, it is true, acted unjustly and absurdly; he has, for a while, protracted my happiness, but to destroy it wholly was beyond his capacity, though not his wishes; and since I have partly succeeded in undermining his project, within some few, some very few days, I shall be blessed with my tender and affectionate Roncorone!

"And are you such, dear friend? You were both when last I saw you; and I hope you have not since changed like the thoughtless ones of this uncertain world! If you have, farewel, first and only man of my love! Retire from me for ever; pity me, if you do not esteem me; use not the tones of ridicule when you speak of me, nor suffer the companions of your mirthful hours to sport with my name, as they would with that of a woman deserving of contumacy for her follies and inconsistencies. Yet why this caution to Roncorone? To him who has spoken so nobly, looked so tenderly, sighed over my misfortunes, vowed affection, and who is so widely known to be the son of Truth and Virtue.

"Oh Rosolie! thou art unjust, and thy suspicions are slanderous. Pardon her, Roncorone, pardon her for these unworthy thoughts! She must be judged by thee; but when thou findest that her very sin springs from the ardent love she bears for thee, it shall only serve to give a milder tone to the words—"Thou art freely pardoned!""

"Perhaps you were not at Venice when I wrote to you; perhaps you are not there now. Are you yet uncertain of my fate?—Are you seeking for me? Unfortunate indeed if neither of my letters shall reach you! You may be ill; incapable of coming to me; pressing the bed of sickness! Good God! how am I tortured by conjectures! Let me suppose that you *did* receive my letter; but then, the tears that fell on it might blot out the place which I mentioned as that of my captivity. I will now, however, be more circumstantial, so as to prevent future mistakes, if any have before arisen."

"The village in which the house stands, is called ————." [Here a word had been written, but it was erased, and no other put in its place. I shivered with the fear of fresh villany, and continued to read with dread.]—"It is a remote and solitary place, and may be wholly unknown to you; I am informed that it is three leagues from the town of ————" [Another erasure, and another shaking of my frame succeeded.]—"Salvini visits no person, nor does he appear to have any society or acquaintance around him; nobody demands admittance at his door, out of which he often passes, though poor Bianca, who, kind creature! is much recovered, and myself never see beyond the mountain on which stands the little village of ————. [Here several words were purposely defaced by blots, beneath which nothing was visible.—'Execrable villain!' I exclaimed; 'for this new insult I will deal out to you a double portion of vengeance.'—It was some time before I could look at the remainder of the letter, which ran thus:—]

"And now, dear Roncorone, having given you these full directions, which I have been enabled to do by the kindness of the servant who favours my correspondence with you, let me, Oh! let me live in the fond expectation of seeing you ere many days shall have passed away. If you should not appear, a thousand forebodings will lie upon my mind; I shall conjecture what I dare not repeat, and Salvini then, I fear, will triumph over my subdued spirit. But let him exult; let him smile on the state to which he shall have reduced me: yet never, never shall he bring me to his purpose of making me his wife, though there should be no alternative between that and death. His wife! I would wrap myself in a shroud, and patiently await the most lingering dissolution of body before I would consent to it.

"Bianca has been commissioned to speak to me in behalf of her brother: but she was a feeble and an unwilling proxy; she pleaded by compulsion, and while she was conversing with me, her agitation was even greater than mine: she sobbed on the bosom which she feared to wound; and seeing my distress, declared that nothing should ever again induce her to enter upon so hateful a subject. She is a worthy creature, and I often mourn that she should be dependant on a morose brother. Roncorone, my humble friend could procure only one sheet of paper to-day; for that, however, I was truly grateful, and I doubt not but that you will be the same when you receive these further assurances of my health and affection.—How I love the good fellow who will forward this to you! He ventures every thing for me. Should the slightest suspicion arise within the mind of his master, he would be driven to beggary. This he has hinted to me; he has also informed me that he has a wife on a sick bed at Venice, with several helpless children around her; and that he can scarcely supply them with the means of subsistence. Almost all the money I could command, I have given to him; when you and I meet, he shall not be forgotten—when we meet!—My grief is returning—Heaven bless you, Roncorone, and direct you in safety to your affectionate

"ROSOLIE."

Such was the composition of the second letter of my beloved girl;—of my feelings on this occasion I shall only say, that they alternately rose from love and rage; that I was now melting into tenderness, and then treading almost on the verge of madness.—The infernal project of Salvini and his minion agonized and confounded me; I could not find curses enough for them; and I could have regarded the elder devils with more respect and charity than these fiendlike mortals. The audacity of the principal agent I thought wonderful, and apprehended that he meant I should never see him again; for I could not suppose that he would have the temerity to encounter with me after such base and unprecedented conduct on his part. This, however, was a chilling reflection, and served to place a world between me and my Rosolie. If I did not admit this conjecture, many things would appear stranger than they had done before. Why did he suffer those tender passages, which were so sweetly expressive of her affection, to remain? Why not strike out those parts which related to Bianca, and threw a most odious shade upon his character? And why not obliterate the sentences in which his name was mentioned with disgust and contempt, and which placed his wintry passion in a ridiculous point of view?

These were mysteries which I could not expound; his plans appeared as awkward as they were malicious, and as inconsistent as they were villanous. My disappointment and misery he evidently aimed at; but, at the same time, he had not, with that species of cunning which characterizes many of the baser composition, endeavoured to heighten my distress, by casting the rainbow colours of success upon his own projects, or by contrasting my defeat with his own victory.—I began to fear that the world contained not another man so dangerous, treacherous, and hypocritical. I almost felt a sorrow to think that the sword of my father did not reach his heart, and empty it of its corrupted blood. For Rosolie I shuddered; poor Bianca, too, was an object of my concern; and I doubted not but that the insults they had received, would be increased tenfold, since their oppressor had possessed himself of the letters of the former, which were sure to make the sentiments and actions of the latter, contrary and opposite to his own, fully known to him.

Repeating the vow of enmity and revenge, I swore, whenever we met again, to deal out to him an ample portion of vengeance; that the injuries of Rosolie, of Bianca, and of myself should be all consolidated and answered for at one time, and on one account.— Scarcely sensible of the tenor of my actions, I hastened to the house in which Alberti resided; I wanted to impart to him my new distresses; but, on enquiring for him, learned that he had gone from Venice in the morning, to be absent several days, and not left any direction behind him.

I thought his absenting himself from me at a time like this, and when he was apprized of the state of my mind, was in some degree unfriendly; for we had been such free participaters of mutual joys and sorrows, that I was now more sensibly affected by his conduct, though in a happier season I should not have noticed it; and I was so unjust and precipitate as to accuse him of instability.—But on my return home I had cause to be ashamed of my suspicions, to make a speedy recantation, and to regard my suspected associate as one of the most worthy of my fellows, as my most assiduous and active friend on earth. I blushed at the meanness of my thoughts, and was vexed by their illiberality, when a letter, written by him, and directed to his "dear friend Roncorone," was delivered to me by my servant. I had still further cause for repentance when I read it; I had also cause to quiet my sorrows, and to take the flatterer, Hope, often as I had been her dupe, again to my bosom; for Alberti informed me that he thought he had found a clue leading to Salvini's retreat—that, knowing my impetuosity, and not being wholly certain of the truth of the report which had been given him, he had been unwilling to send me forward in a search that was as likely to be ended with disappointment as with success.

"The distance I am going," he said, "is not very great: expect my return in the course of a few days; but, if it be prolonged to a week, be not unnecessarily concerned.—When I see you again, Roncorone, be prepared to receive happy intelligence with a temperate pleasure, or an account of my unsuccess with fortitude. Scarcely half an hour has elapsed since I obtained the slender information on which I am beginning my pursuit; to serve you, my friend, my brother, I am ever anxious; two of the elements I would at any time traverse for your sake; a third I would brave for your preservation; and though in the other I have no possible capacity, yet the animating spirit of intellect should follow you even thither, restless still to communicate and to be familiar with you. I go, Roncorone;—Prosperity, waft me thy gales to the nearest shore, and afterwards attend me in the paths which I may tread."

A person inclined to superstition, and experiencing such a rapid succession of painful and pleasing events, might have supposed that the good and ill spirits of the invisible worlds were contending to whose power he should be subject, and by whom controuled. Though I was less extravagant in my imagination, yet I thought the occurrences which pressed on me were most extraordinary and uncommon;—how they might terminate was a perplexing mystery; but I was willing to believe that happiness—Ah! man is ever an egregious dupe, the dupe even of himself!

A father wishes not to see his first unborn offspring more than I did to see Alberti. He was not returned on the fifth day after his departure; he did not come back on the sixth. When at home, I was continually looking from the door and the windows; if I were walking in the streets, my eyes examined every passenger, and were directed into every carriage, in the hope of encountering the expected messenger; and I heard not the dashing of an oar without wishing that it were assisting in bringing my friend to me. On the eighth day he was in my arms! I looked hastily in his face; it was animated, beaming with pleasure; success shone through his eyes; and as I strained him closer to my breast, I found his heart beating the lively tune of joy.

"Is she found?" I enquired, with a rapid voice.

"She is found," he replied.

"Thank God! thank God!" I exclaimed, sinking from his embrace, and bursting into tears. Alberti did not coldly check the impulse, but, by his sweetly sorrowful eyes, I saw that his electric soul had caught those emotions which flew from mine.

"Be tranquil, dear Roncorone," he cried, after a pause of some minutes; "be tranquil, and listen to what I have to say. I bring you tidings of happiness, not of sorrow."

"My agitation," I replied, "is not the effect of sorrow; it is caused by the too sudden burst of joy, but it is going over. Tell me of my Rosolie, and all will be well: begin, begin, my friend—I am wholly prepared."

"On the morning that I left Venice," he said, "I was talking with the Count di Castello, and amongst other topics the disappearance of Salvini was introduced. The subject indeed had, within the last few days, become very general; and expressing my surprise at so private an occurrence, and saying I could wish to know to what part of the country he had withdrawn himself, the Count informed me that a friend of his had very recently, from the window of an inn, seen Salvini walking in the streets of Trent, though, from the simplicity of his dress, and altered garb, the observer did not at first recognize him. I seemed to listen to this intelligence without any great degree of concern, though I was at the same time much interested, and highly busied in forming a project, even while the Count, who, you know, is but a toilet butterfly, was indulging himself, and, as he thought, gratifying me, with the vapid amours and idle garbage of affected libertinism. I broke from him, however, as soon as possible, and hastened towards my home. In my way thither I passed by the door of Salvini's house, from which I saw a porter going with a hamper on his shoulders; and as I walked behind him in the street, perceived a direction in large characters on it, to Signor Castlevetro at Trent. 'This is probably the assumed name of Roncorone's enemy; this may perhaps lead me to a discovery of something worth seeking for.'—So I said to myself, as I went homewards, being fully resolved, within that very hour, to leave Venice, and search for Salvini at the place to which the Count had referred me, and to which this discovery also pointed."

"I thank you from my soul!" I cried;—"pray proceed."

"I knew that uncertainty would accompany me in my route, and therefore would not ask you to join me in it; I thought that another serious disappointment of hopes so repeatedly created and extinguished, would be too weighty for your philosophy; and as my expectations and apprehensions were nearly equal, I conceived it to be more prudent to keep you in a short suspense at home, than to carry you a considerable distance from it, when the accomplishing of my purposes was so very precarious."

"It was kindly thought, my generous Alberti; go on, I beseech you."

"Having written my note, and dispatched it to you, in a few minutes after I was on the water, and in less than two hours was put on shore. I then began my journey, and after several perplexing delays and difficulties, arrived at Trent, where I immediately commenced my enquiries: the name of Castlevetro was not, however, known by any person to whom I applied, though I was directed to a barber whose appellation differed only in one letter. It was from the postmaster I learned that a packet, directed to Signor Castlevetro, had been sent to the house; that a person had called and taken it from thence, and desired, that in case any others should arrive, that they might be forwarded by a courier to him at B———, a remote village about eight miles distant from Trent. A description of his person highly flattered me that it was Salvini; but preferring facts to conjectures, I went forward to the place which the postmaster had mentioned, a very obscure spot among the mountains, to find which I was compelled to engage

a guide, who brought me to it just at the close of day. I was conducted to a wretched inn, and the first person I saw there was the
rascally servant of Salvini, mentioned by Rosolie in her letter; my
indignation rising, I was strangely tempted to squeeze the villain's
throat; but prudence forbade it, and I walked, with my face nearly
hidden, through the room in which he was sitting, desiring my
host to conduct me to the chamber in which I was to sleep—a
place tenanted by vermin, and most vilely scented. The landlord
had scarcely withdrawn when I heard the voice of the hypocritical scoundrel, with which I was well acquainted, enquiring how
much he had to pay, and saying that he was obliged to depart, as
his master would be expecting him in half an hour. From this it
was evident that Salvini's residence was not far distant; it was clear
and satisfactory that my pursuit had not been vain, and therefore,
when the landlord brought up my odious supper, I asked no questions, in order that I might create no suspicions."

"You were perfectly consistent," said I; "but my Rosolie! pray
go on."

"I was undetermined in respect to what I should further do in
this business. I wished to go boldly to Salvini, to make your injuries my own, and to bring back your Rosolie with me to Venice;
but I thought it probable that, if I incensed Salvini, he would
defeat the whole of my project, by a more obstinate seclusion of
the principal object; and also that I might rouse the beast, without
being able to subdue it. I determined, therefore, privately in the
morning, to leave the village, hasten back to you with all possible
speed, and leave you to act as your judgment might prompt you. I
have done so, and hope you approve my conduct."

"Approve! I cannot tell you how much I am indebted to you,"
I replied; "I cannot explain to you the nature of my heart's gratitude; it is superior to any thing that I ever before felt for benefits
received.—Within this hour will I leave Venice, and pursue the
path which you have lately trodden:—happy, happy Roncorone,
to find that it will lead to Rosolie. Alberti, I will not request you
to accompany me; I would not make you an object of Salvini's
malice, and I confess I wish to meet my dear girl alone: on my
return, however, I shall expect to see you, and also that you will
be present at the nuptials of me and Rosolie, which I shall press to

have immediately performed. You find that I make sure of obtaining her: Salvini *shall* deliver her up; he shall resign either her or his life; and even when I have released her from his power, his insolence and contumacy must be accounted for."

"Proceed to no violence," said my friend; "spare the reptile when it is no longer venomous."

He gave me some further cautions, which I listened to, and generally approved. At parting, he wished and assured me of success, and very soon after I set out on my design.

* * * * * *

Would you, stranger, have a circumstantial account of my journey? I will give it to you if my wits allow me; but if they should fail, I cannot account for inconsistencies.

Though the distance to Trent seemed long, yet the way to it was pleasant. I met no travellers whose faces I thought looked more lively than my own: none appeared to go forward with so much ardour; none, I conceived, expected to find so precious a treasure at the different places of their destination. So near to my Rosolie! within a few miles—My heart was almost bursting from my bosom, and the excess of my joy more than once betrayed me into tears.

I rested only a few hours at Trent, and then went forward, as directed by Alberti; but as it was early day, I relied on receiving necessary information across the mountains, and therefore did not then provide myself with a guide. After leaving the town, however, I found the road more difficult than I had supposed it to be, and was obliged to hire a director to shew me across one or two of the eminences; but as soon as he pointed out to me the brow of a hill, which he described as rising immediately above the village to which I was going, I dismissed him with an ample reward, because my feelings were making me unfit for his observance.

I could not, at a time like this, pay much regard to either the beauties or the wonders of nature, though the spot was entirely new to me. The mountains wore gigantic forms; but an advanced spring had made them, in many parts, beautiful, lively, and refreshing to the eye; the highest of them, however, in spite of the approaches of summer, still stubbornly retained their hoods of snow, coyly refusing to yield to the influence of the sun, though they could neither withdraw themselves from his notice, nor shun the daily courtship of his rays.

Still nearer to my Rosolie—separated from her only by one hill! I was most anxious to reach its summit, and improved my pace, after having left my tired horse at a little inn, which I supposed to be the same where my friendly Alberti had seen the pretended assistant of Rosolie. My blood now seemed to flow more rapidly, and I could scarcely regulate my passions; I began to disregard the cautions which Alberti had given me, in respect to my conduct on seeing Salvini, and thought it scarcely possible to meet that unworthy being without bestowing on him more than reproaches. I resolved, however, that the state in which I found Rosolie should determine every thing; I conjectured what the state of her mind was, and thought that it would require to be soothed, rather than to be again disturbed.

While I was thus thinking, a horse rushed with uncommon violence past me, furious, and not to be governed by its rider; the softness of the turf had prevented me from hearing its approach, nor did I notice it till its affrighted eyes and bristling mane were within a few yards of me. The velocity of the beast was so great, that I could scarcely distinguish the sex of the person mounted on it; it left its foam behind as it madly tore up the ground that lay before it; I dreaded the fate of the horseman, and thinking his death inevitable, my breath failed me almost as much as his own could do. My eyes followed the animal nearly a quarter of a mile; when, shuddering, I saw it take a furious leap from the brow of the hill, which I concluded to be the death-deed of itself, and of the person who disappeared along with it.

Feeling the different impulses of humanity and terror, I ran forward, and was soon at the spot where the steed and the man had sunk from my view; it was a frightful abyss! my eye no sooner beheld it than it recoiled, and my head, when I hung it over the brink of the precipice, instantly became giddy. I retreated a few steps, but returned almost immediately, and again looked down the horrid chasm, which, though immensely deep, was light even at the bottom. No human step could possibly have ever trodden within it; my imagination dwelt on it as on the residence of gnomes, and of those supernatural agents who, according to vulgar opinion, assemble at midnight to plot the destruction of man. Only one of its sides had a small projection; the other was so perpendicular, that a pebble dropped from the brink, would have reached the base without, in any degree, deviating.

I was obliged to lie flat on the earth to have a distinct view of the cave; this was the first time that I discovered there was satisfaction in terror, for I found a difficulty in raising my eyes, and felt an instinct to give myself up a victim to the mouth of the pit, as the surprised bird does to the jaws of the rattle-snake. I saw the carcase of the horse lying nearly at the end opposite that at which I had placed myself; its neck was twisted entirely round, its body burst, and its loosened bowels, strewed upon the earth, were smoking at the bottom, and sending a thin vapour midway of the chasm. Discovering no vestiges of the man, I concluded that he had been dashed to atoms; but at that moment I heard a doleful cry, and looking around me, perceived him miraculously suspended by his garments on the only bush that grew from the side of the precipice, with his head downwards, and supported in the most fragile state that can possibly be conceived.

I was on the rack to extricate him from a situation so singularly shocking, so unlike any thing that I had ever seen or imagined, and the truth of which, had it been related to me, I should not have been inclined to admit; but no means presented themselves, and I still considered him as doomed to certain destruction, and to an agonizing death. Within a few minutes, however, I saw a short and very narrow ridge of earth leading to the spot; but as it looked of a crumbling nature, and admitted scarcely the breadth of my feet, I found great danger in treading it, and for a moment desisted from the attempt. The suspended wretch calling in tones of distraction for assistance, I hesitated no longer, but ventured to walk upon the unsolid earth, though my head seemed to whirl upon my shoulders as I advanced.

I was soon within a yard or two of him:—I could not reach him with my arm, nor was I rash enough to attempt it; but taking off my upper garment, I grasped one part of it firmly, and told him to catch at the other;—he aimed at it several times, and at length successfully, when I opposed my whole strength to his weight, but expected each moment to descend with him to the bottom of the cave. Though I am now meagre and spectre-like, and though almost all my marrow has distilled from my bones, yet at that time I had a vigour equal to that of almost any man, a body as firmly compacted, and an arm as well nerved. My efforts were most ardent; I had the life of a man to redeem—probably of a worthy and an excellent man!—a husband, a father! My power increased; the ground remained solid; and I drew him to my feet; his clothes were spread over his face; and finding that he was nearly fainting, I dragged him cautiously after me, pulled him to a safe spot of earth, and setting him upright against my body, threw the covering from his head.

"Salvini!" I exclaimed, in astonishment, and drawing myself from him.

"Roncorone!" he cried, with a blackened and distorted face; "is it you—*you* to whom I owe my life?"

"I have preserved it, Signor, and am pleased with the event, though you have shewn yourself my bitterest enemy, and though your actions have been mean and contemptible."

"And I scarcely think my preservation a blessing, when I consider by whom it was effected. Had I known who was extricating me from my danger, I would almost as readily have leaped into death, as to have accepted your assistance."

"Ingrate!" I exclaimed, "I want no thanks; give them to Heaven; render them to God, to whom I am only an humble agent. Your life, as it is, is a worthless thing preserved; mend it, and I may think the moment in which I rescued you fortunate and happy."

"Roncorone," he replied, "preach not to me in the strains of affected humility;—the counterfeit will not pass. You knew me before you stretched out your arm to my assistance, and in serving me you looked for a latent reward, and thought that I should more readily attend to your supplications."

"Supplications! Supplications to *you!*—the idea excites my mirth; and though I have lately shuddered at your pending fate, almost provokes me to laughter."

"Leave me," he cried; "withdraw, and indulge the propensity

apart from me. I never can respect either you, or any one bearing your name. Leave me, I repeat, and never see me more!"

"Be not so hasty, Signor," I said; "the compassion which I felt for you is changed into disgust, and my concern and sympathy have given place to contempt and indifference. I look on you with astonishment; you appear to me something more depraved than I conceived human nature possibly could be; and I almost think that I ventured too greatly in your rescue. Had I redeemed the horse that carried you over the brink, I might have perceived in him as much gratitude."

"I could have blessed and rewarded any other man for the action; but *you*——"

"What of me, Signor?"

"You are baneful to my sight: your father, before you were born, was my bitterest enemy."

"Admitting that he were, am I, at this time, to be censured for it? But he only chastised you for cruelty, insolence, and presumption. That action which humiliated you, gave a trait of greatness to his character."

" 'Tis well," said Salvini, rising from the ground; "boast on till you are weary: from this moment I will never see you again."

"Stay!" I cried, catching hold of his arm; "stay, attempt not to go if you value your life. Do you suppose that I meet with you now by accident? You have provoked me, Salvini, and I tell you—you are a villain."

"A villain! a villain!"

"Aye, a petty contemptible villain!—You have done me wrong, and shall answer for it. Why did you oppose my union with Venzone's daughter? Why force her from Venice? Why detain her against her will? and why, pitiful being, intercept her letters, alter the form of them, and send them as new insults to me?"

"Have I done *all* these things?" he said, with extreme agitation.

"You have, you have! Every thing that is base and rancorous are you capable of performing. But your machinations have been defeated, your haunts explored, and your evil designs discovered in a happy season. Do you not tremble at your detection?"

"Tremble? No, no!"

"You do, coward! your limbs are quaking, your cheeks

colourless; the marks of guilt and of fear are upon your face. But I have now no time to parley: I am come to remove a dear and beloved object from your oppression; yield up to me Venzone's daughter, or your body shall be breathless before night!"

"I will not yield her up—by Heaven I will not!"

"You *shall*, brave Signor; you shall resign her to me, and immediately too. I came purposely to convey her hence, and will not be disappointed, though you should get thousands to oppose me. You love her, Signor! you have poured your vows into her ear! you would plant a delicate flower in the frozen soil of winter! But it will not do, Salvini! Prudence, at your age, might have taught you better."

He looked at me with a most malicious aspect, and walked hastily away; but I followed him closely, kept near his heels, and regulated my paces according to his own.—His villany and ingratitude had roused me, and enlarged my veins; I could scarcely restrain myself from laying the hands of violence on him, and almost fancied that I was pursuing a fiend, who had merely assumed the human shape and habit. Several times he turned round, and told me to retire from him: but my project was formed; I was resolved to take Rosolie from him that very day, and informed him so when he desired me to desist. His countenance now began to vary; it was alternately white and crimson; he quickened his pace; I likewise improved mine, and in about a quarter of an hour we arrived at his house.

Casting my eyes up to a window, I saw my Rosolie! I heard her scream with joy; the sound thrilled my soul, but I could only hold up my hand to her, as Salvini was then entering at the door. Rushing into the hall, he desired that I might be prevented from following him, and the servants were gathering round me; but my words and actions convinced them that I was too resolute and strong for their purpose, and therefore they did not offer to touch me. Enraged and almost frenzied, Salvini went into a small room, and with an assumed composure I accompanied him thither; though my heart was anxious to be near my Rosolie, I restrained my impatience as much as possible, and endeavoured to be calm and collected in my dealings with my implacable enemy, whose fury was increasing every moment, and who, after a short silence, was preparing to leave the room.

Conjecturing what his designs were, I told him that, wherever he went, I would follow him, unless he gave Rosolie immediately up to me, and allowed us to depart from him together; but this served only to increase his irritation, and, in his frenzy, he flew towards a pistol, which was lying on a table at the other end of the room. Noticing the premeditated action, I rushed upon him, and in an instant wrested the weapon from his grasp. Finding, however, that it was not loaded, I threw it indignantly at his feet, and smiled at the frustration of his brutality and malice.

"Would you turn murderer, wretch?" I exclaimed; "would you stain yourself with blood, to make your resemblance to a dæmon still more complete?"

"Leave the house," he cried, "instantly leave the house! You shall repent this insolence, Roncorone; be assured that I will be revenged."

"I have nothing to fear, Signor," I replied; "there are few men by whose threats I could be alarmed; but those which come from slackening manhood are apt to excite laughter, rather than to create in me alarm.—Be sparing, therefore, of your invectives, and hear me with patience."

"I will not hear you; I will hear nothing."

"Nay, but you shall, Signor; I no longer solicit, I demand. Of your baseness and hypocrisy I shall say no more; conscience may hereafter scourge you when I shall be far distant. The purport of my errand is to tell you that Rosolie is no longer your ward. Your power as a guardian ceases from this hour; from this hour she is mine."

"Ideally so," said Salvini with a sneer.

"Actually so!" exclaimed Rosolie, entering the room, and rushing into my anxious arms.

What a moment was that! Surely my sensations were as exquisite as those felt by an angel on seeing the spirit of a worldly friend newly arrived in the realms of Heaven! Ye who have loved, may fancy it. Sainted woman! the remembrance of that happy period makes my heart——Oh! surely the blood is gushing from it!—Ah, my wife! my martyred wife!"

* * * * * *

I have yielded to my sorrows four days—it has calmed me—I am now able to proceed.

"Roncorone!" said Rosolie, placing her head upon my breast, regardless of the presence of Salvini.

"My love!" I exclaimed; "my Rosolie!"

"Oh how happy is this meeting!" she sweetly murmured.

"Blessed! it is blessed!" I replied, straining her still closer to my bosom. Salvini had sunk, as if overpowered by surprise and vexation, into a chair; he eyed us sternly, and looked as if he could willingly be our murderer.

"Will you go with me now, Rosolie?" I enquired; "will you accompany me from hence?"

"Readily," she replied; "give me only a few moments to speak to Signor Salvini."

She walked up to him with firmness, and I went with her, holding her hand within mine.

"Signor," she cried, "perhaps this is the last time we shall ever see each other; for I confess that I shall never be induced to solicit a subsequent interview. There was a time when the idea of leaving you would have been painful; but now I shall fly from, and continue to avoid you as a most dangerous and cruel enemy. I regard the changes of your character with astonishment—I add, with disgust. Good Heaven! you snatched me from danger in my childhood, for several years acted like a kind and benevolent guardian; yet now, you would not only distress, but also involve me in ruin, in shame, and infamy!"

She wept—Salvini trembled—I was enraged, and could scarcely refrain from violence.

"You have given me maintenance and education," continued Rosolie, recovering; "and I have many times thanked and blessed you for it. Your generosity always met with my gratitude; every night you had the prayers of an orphan; every night I supplicated Providence to send you a reward, greater than it was in the power of all the world to bestow. I was not prompted to this by the forms of society; I had a monitor within my breast who told me to do it. Thus far the picture pleases; the other part presents itself dark, gloomy, disgustful!"

"You are in a fine declamatory strain this morning!" said Salvini, between savageness and irony.

"Signor," she replied, "the arrows of your satire can no longer wound me, my heart is now become invulnerable to such attacks, though a few hours ago you had me so much within your power. When we lose all manner of respect for an object, it is not long before we can totally disregard it; the esteem which I once entertained for you exists no longer, and your name and character I shall soon give to forgetfulness.—Why you forced me from Venice, I shall not now enquire; neither shall I ask why you have since harassed, perplexed, and insulted me. Let me, however, inform you, that two nights ago I became acquainted with the low expedients you made use of to intercept my letters; you, and the vile being who delivered them to you, were very communicative in the garden; you did not feel any humiliation, at that time, in converting with the sorriest wretch on earth, a contemptible liar, and plotting villain. You laughed, Signor, at your successes; I heard it all from the window of a room into which, though forbidden, I had entered; I heard also the plan of your premeditated designs and treacherous intentions!"

"What designs?" said I, starting; "what intentions, my Rosolie?"

"They are frustrated, Roncorone," she replied, "most happily frustrated by your appearance; therefore enquire not concerning them. What I have suffered, forget; what I may hereafter suffer through enmity, resent as love and honour shall prompt you. Signor," she continued, turning to Salvini, "before I go, I will openly explain to you my intentions: my heart is, as I have often told you, attached to Signor Roncorone; nor do I blush to add, that I wish to be united to him. Your reasons for impeding such an union are of a feathery substance;—and even if you had in your possession the paper which, on a former occasion, you mentioned to have been deposited by the hands of my dying parent, yet the written request of a father (incompetent at that time to judge of my future circumstances), who has been so many years in the earth, shall not destroy or vary those principles on which I now ground virtue and happiness."

"Are you the daughter of Venzone?" said Salvini.

"Are you the friend of Venzone's daughter?" cried Rosolie, with indignation; "Signor, recollect! Did you not throw aside that character last night? Did you not—good Heaven! did you not, resembling a fiend rather than a man, last night——"

"What of last night?" I exclaimed, interrupting her; "what of last night, Rosolie?"

"Nothing, Roncorone," she replied;—"come, I will go with you. Signor, I am parting from you for ever."

"Salvini," I cried, "if ever we meet again, I shall wish to see more honourable characters in your face, and to discover more generous sentiments in your mind, more virtue in your heart."

"Beware!" he said, "beware of what that mind, and of what that heart may suggest! Beware of what these hands may execute!"

"Boast and vanity!" I exclaimed;—"vaunts of imbecility! Rosolie, my arm; let us be gone this instant; let us fly from this residence of malice and vice."

Salvini was rushing upon her, in order to prevent her going; but I put him aside with my arm, and led her out of the room. He had brought with him from Venice only two servants; such force, therefore, as there was to oppose me, I could have resisted. The rascal who had been the deceiver and robber of Rosolie, did not now appear, concealing himself, perhaps, through dread of receiving the punishment he so well deserved. The other domestic made a faint resistance when we were passing the door; but taking hold of his shoulders, I drove him to the opposite wall, and then walked on with my sweet Rosolie, regardless of the curses which Salvini sent after us. I now beheld her as mine!—My joy was almost too great; and when we lost sight of the house, I stopped, and pressed her with rapture to my heart. She smiled, wept, and talked of our future happiness.

"But what of last night?" I said; "what of last night, my love?"

"Salvini was insolent."

"What, rude? Was he rude?"

"Yes, Roncorone, he came upon me by surprise."

"Villain!—I'll murder him!"

My blood seemed to run like lava, and I wanted to return, in order that I might crush his carcase into dust; but Rosolie held me

by the arm, smiled away my rage, and made me promise not to
think of revenge.—Would I had not listened to her! would I had
met him again, and cut out the heart of the rank villain from his
accursed body! * * *

* * * * * *

I remembered the path I had taken from the inn, and it was
not long before I returned to it with the dear prize for which I had
been a fortunate adventurer. The distance was not long, and therefore occasioned her scarcely any fatigue; but, as I had conjectured,
there was no horse to be procured to take her on her way to Trent,
though I was informed that I might probably be accommodated at
a house which was named to be within two miles. Rosolie, feeling
herself secure under my protection, smiled at this little perplexity,
and assured me that she should be able to walk to the place which
our host had mentioned, and even from thence to Trent, provided
the means of conveyance could not be then met with.

"Surely, on such an occasion as this," she said, gaily, "I may
exert myself a little, particularly if I think that, had you not arrived
till to-morrow, I should have perhaps been driven from you for
ever."

"Why that suspicion, my lovely Rosolie?"

"Because it was the intention of the Signor to depart from
hence tomorrow, and to take me and Bianca with him to France.
This design he communicated to me, though I had previously
and secretly been made acquainted with it by the conversation
which had been held between him and his despicable servant in
the garden, and which, as I have before told you, I heard from a
window of one of the chambers. A few hours more, Roncorone,
and I should have been driven from you into a foreign country,
where I should have been the victim of insolence, and perhaps of
rudeness."

"Cursed beyond redemption," I exclaimed, "might he have
been who dared to offer it!"

"Salvini, I fear," she said, "would have been that villain; after
what I have lately seen of him, I should have had every thing that
is shocking and brutal continually to dread. This is the man who,

over the death-bed of my father, vowed to protect his helpless child! But let us talk no more of him; he is unworthy, Roncorone, therefore let us forget him. You are my confidence, my hope of felicity! While I am in the possession of your love, so long shall I be happy."

"Be happy then, sweet Rosolie!" I cried, folding her in my arms; "be happy till the hour in which death shall separate us; till the last moment of mortality; till one of us join the shadows of the departed, leaving the other with painful reluctance and regret."

She melted into tears, and sunk upon my breast; my sensibility was likewise affected; it prevented me from speaking further, and for a few moments we both remained silent. The landlord coming in, I desired him to lead my horse to the door; which being afterwards done, I placed Rosolie upon it, and led it by the bridle to the other inn, to which we had been directed, where we fortunately procured a carriage, and an additional horse to take us to Trent, at which place we arrived in the evening.

The spirits of my Rosolie now reviving, she appeared to me more lovely and interesting than ever; the hours which we spent till we retired to our beds, were hours of delight and of happiness; our past dangers and difficulties were either forgotten, or slightly mentioned; her love was aided by her confidence in me, and mine, sincere and tender, rested on the foundation of honour. We talked unreservedly of our approaching union: we formed such plans of joy—but Oh! few of them were realized!

On the following morning we left the town, and proceeded in a more comfortable manner towards Venice, which place we arrived at in due course of time, and in perfect safety. My first care was to place my Rosolie in the little house that I had prepared for her previously to the commencement of our perplexities, the possession of which the servants whom I had hired still retained;—I then went to seek for Alberti; nor was I long in finding him. Rushing into his arms, I rapidly told him of my successes, and his congratulations were neither few nor tardy.

"Did I not tell you," he cried, "that Prosperity would attend you if you did but smile on her? From this time, Roncorone, knit not your brows on the trifling embarrassments of life, or on the contrarieties of worldly circumstances. But indeed I am most happy that you have recovered the possession of the sweet Venzone."

"It is you," I cried, "it is you, Alberti, to whom I owe her! Had it not been for your friendly solicitude and assiduity, she would probably have been kept apart from me for a long time—perhaps for ever!"

"Let me be repaid by my own pleasure, rather than by your thanks," replied Alberti. "But what of Salvini? What have you to say of him?"

"That he is a villain is too little to report, too favourable; that the earth bears not one more atrocious, comes nearer to the truth. I will, however, speak of him as we go along; for my love will be impatient at my delay, and on this happy day I cannot dispense with your society."

"I took him by his arm, and we went out together, and returned to Rosolie with all possible expedition. I had already apprized her of the very friendly services of Alberti, and particularly mentioned the readiness and promptitude with which he had undertaken the journey to discover Salvini's retreat.—Gratitude always makes the aspect sweet; but it rendered Rosolie's lovely and fascinating;—and when she received the salutation of my friend, her animated features, her smiles, and her soft accents caused me to adore her, if it were possible, more than ever, and apparently made a captive of Alberti.

Having been for so long a time previous to this the sport and derision of mischance, I could scarcely regulate my actions, or limit my joy. Rosolie was, in some degree, actuated by similar affections; and the spirits of Alberti, seldom depressed, were now in perfect harmony: the day therefore was exquisitely passed by our little society, and it was at a late hour when I and Alberti departed from the house.

"Is she not amiable?" I enquired, almost as soon as the door was closed; "is she not a lovely being?"

"She is delectable!" he replied; "a poet, in describing her, might possibly be extravagant; but he would be obliged, in justice, to enrich his image with the choicest ornaments. Joy to you, my Roncorone; joy to you, I repeat, on the acquisition of so exquisite a partner!"

The cold prudential mortal deals out his maxims with precision, and sends forth his frigid sentiments, struck, like inferior coin, from the mint of his drossy brain; but I was discoursing with an almost brother on the tenderest of all subjects; therefore, whatever rose within my mind, my tongue scrupled not to express, nor did caution privately hint to me that I was garrulous. After I had parted from Alberti, I was little inclined to sleep; for joy had banished the usual torpor of the mind. Though I sought for Rosolie early the next day, she was risen before I arrived, and ran forward to meet me as I entered at the door; her looks expressed happiness and tranquillity, and she gave me the morning salutation with vivacity.

She was greatly pleased with the little habitation I had chosen for her, and commended every preparation I had made; she thanked me for my love and delicacy, and gazed with a bright eye upon my portrait; my literary arrangement she said was good, and my musical selections were not less admired.—She approved of the man and woman who were to attend us—she was happy—her wishes were gratified.

The season was delightful, and the breezes, which came across the waves of the Adriatic, allayed the heats of summer; the flowers of our little garden were beautiful to the eye, and sweet to the scent, and its simple alcoves were inviting. Rosolie promised to be mine at the end of a week; there was *then* the most perfect union of soul, nor could customary ceremonies make it more complete.

The limited time went over, and she became my wife! Heaven never heard more sincere vows than our's were: had God been visible to mine eye, I could not have spoken more truly; and I most devoutly thanked him for the blessing he then bestowed on me. Ah, Roncorone! Grief is too potent for your resistance.

* * * * * *

We had no idle visiters to disturb our quiet; our marriage was indeed talked of in Venice, and some few of our former acquaintances were induced to seek us in our retirement;—those who, we conceived, were really prompted by friendship, we admitted; but to those who, we suspected, came merely to gape and be impertinent, we were denied. Our door was always open to our friend

Alberti, and we were ever glad to see him; Rosolie's respect for him was equal to mine, and from him we had a lively account of almost every occurrence in Venice;—but so whimsical was the narrator, that he frequently jumbled together the affairs of the Senate and of the Opera, and passed, in an instant, from the most serious concerns of the Republic to the description of a new ballet. His musical talent was a recommendation to the favour of Rosolie; and his spirits, being uninterruptedly good, he would either play or sing whenever requested.

To our great surprise, Alberti informed us that Salvini was returned to, and publicly appearing in Venice; that he was undaunted at the sarcastic remarks which were made on his conduct, and hypocritically and most strenuously endeavouring to alter the opinion which had been so generally formed of his recent proceedings. In order to accomplish this purpose, he was spreading stories, wherever he went, highly prejudicial to me and Rosolie; but Alberti led me to suppose that they were suspectingly received, and that the present artifices of my enemy were too ill-contrived and feeble to bring back his reputation to its former standard.

Provoked at these fresh proofs of his insolence and malice, I felt much inclined to go immediately in search of him, that I might give him the chastisement he had so long merited; but seeing Rosolie terrified when I hinted at such an intention, I did not execute it, though I was enraged to think that the slanderous coward should be left to propagate his infamous lies with impunity.

I however wrote a letter to him, peremptorily desiring him to adhere to truth in whatever he said respecting either me or my wife, and to create no story whereby the world might be able to censure us; if he acted consistently, as I wished, I informed him that I should wholly disregard his future concerns; but if he still persisted in his idleness and depravity, I vowed that I would render him a public spectacle of pain and disgrace.

He did not reply to this letter, nor did I afterwards meet with him when I went occasionally to the city. Alberti informed me that he appeared but little in public, that the austerity of his features was increased, and that the name of his late ward was not so often repeated by him. I conjectured this change to be owing to cowardice, rather than to good principles; and, whatever might have caused it, I could but feel satisfied, as it made my dear Rosolie more happy and tranquil.

* * * * * *

But I am prevented for a while from continuing my narrative; my materials are nearly all wasted, and to obtain a supply is somewhat difficult. Most of these mountaineers are poor and ignorant, which accounts for their honesty;—their superior fellows, if the expression be not absurd, might indeed accommodate me; but I detest to ask a favour of those who are erect and consequential, and who, in their own inverted eyes, appear of such infinite importance, though to the sight of other men, whom they wish to confound, they seem little more than pigmies aiming at the stride and gait of a giant. Oh world, world! of what strange matter art thou composed! To examine thy corrupted particles, most vile and mocking in the mass, may sometimes provoke a smile, but will more often excite a tear. Oh, I am sick and weary of thee!

There is a little peasant boy who, deriding the fears of his associates, for it seems I am an innocent cause of terror, often offers himself to serve me. I think the stripling loves me tenderly; for he is as willing to do me a kindness as if I were a Monarch, and he my page; he smiles in my face when he hears me speak; and in doing what I wish him to perform, he is as active as a kid. He loves not money, though I force him to take it; and tells me that such rewards lessen the pleasure which he feels in obliging me. Early independence of an uncommon soul!

Boy, I judge that thou wilt not be fated to waste thy days in tending a herd upon these mountains; if thou shouldst, may neither blast affect the herbage, nor murrain thy cattle! If thy active spirit lead thee to range the world, may the rays of a protecting Providence fall upon every chosen path!

My young friend promised me yesterday to procure me the materials necessary for continuing my narrative; he could not obtain them in the village, but assured me that it should not be long before I received them.

* * * * * *

My messenger is returned with the paper. He has been three leagues for it; but, in order to prevent any concern on my part, he tells me that he had another errand.

"I wanted to buy a book," he says;—"but it was not to be had at the place I have been to. My mother loves to hear me read, loves to see me happy; she therefore gave me the money which was necessary, and which I will work the harder for, and also allowed me to go to the town where I thought of making my purchase. But for the time I have lost, I can easily make amends, by rising an hour earlier, and working an hour later in every day of next week."

Oh that my misfortunes would allow me to be calm—that, if not happy, I could be tranquil—that my heart were less sick, and my mind not subject to such frenzied emotions as often torture it! Then would I make this stripling my peculiar care, educate him, husband the rich soil of his intellects, and polish the diamond that is so rare and of such native worth. Ah, Roncorone! how canst thou transmit the rays of reason to any one, when thy own mind is either unillumed, or strangely chequered by the various lights of an extravagant imagination?

Boy, I can deliver to thee no precepts, much as I love thee. Thou art, I think, of a more than vulgar mould, but to be wise is not always to be happy; the cultivated mind takes in a thousand ills, receives a thousand inflictions, of which the illiterate would not be sensible. The fool shakes his bells, and is pleased—still if they jingle not, he falls not into melancholy; but the wise man looks for uninterrupted harmony, and a single note of discord frets him as a peal of thunder would a timid and unhoused traveller. Oh worldly wisdom! what a body of absurdities may we find in thee!

* * * * * *

Carry me, befriending memory, back to my pleasant home; to my house of quiet; to the fair being who resided in it, whose heart was my repository, whose bosom was my pillow! Rare composition of all the excellencies of Nature! dear resemblance of what we picture of the spirits of the secret world! Rhapsodist I am none:

stranger, if you had known her, you would neither wonder at my words, nor think them extravagant.

Connubial love, how sweet did I find thee! I and my Rosolie were happy, harmonious, in peace with mankind, and grateful to Heaven. Our retirement was enchanting; and to improve the natural beauties around us, to arrange the blushing flowers in our garden, to cull the sweets of poesy, and to wander in an evening upon the borders of the tranquil sea, gave us more pleasure than we could have found in the active city.

The expectations which I had formed before I possessed her, were fully realized; and great and many as my wishes had been, they were completely answered. Of Venice we saw little; we however heard much of it from Alberti, whose friendship increased, rather than diminished: Salvini was become wholly a stranger to us, and we held little converse with any of his acquaintances.

We were one evening preparing to go on the water, when we were surprised to see a carriage driven up to the door, and the coachman alight, in order to let some person out of it. Rosolie and I went to the window, and in a moment perceived poor Signora Bianca, pale, and apparently weakened by affliction, slowly walking towards the house: we both ran forward to meet her, and my tender Rosolie threw her arms around the neck of her enfeebled friend, who, choked with grief, could not speak to either of us; she, however, took hold of my arm, and when she got into the parlour, sunk on a sofa, and burst into tears.

My wife was greatly affected, and their sorrows touched my heart. Bianca was evidently in agony, for her breath seemed nearly suppressed; and though she endeavoured repeatedly to speak, she could not articulate a single word. Rosolie still conjured her to be composed, and I joined my entreaties to her's; but the grief of our unhappy visiter was absolute, and it was several minutes before she could put any degree of restraint upon it. Her appearance alone was sufficient to excite compassion; for her eyes seemed as if they were losing themselves in their sockets; and her cheeks, colourless and thin, resembled those of a corpse rather than of an animated being.

"I beg you, dear Signora," said Rosolie, "I beg you to be comforted. To see you thus afflicts me greatly: tell me what I can do for you."

"Nothing, Rosolie," she replied; "nothing at present, dear girl! My worldly wants are almost over: look in my face, child; look at my emaciated figure! I am come hither only to die in peace!"

"To die!" exclaimed Rosolie; "to die! God forbid!"

"If you love me, Rosolie," she answered, "you will say, God grant it! You will implore him, as I do, to remove my afflictions, and to quiet for ever the agonizing pulsations of my broken heart; broken by the cruelty of an unnatural brother. Oh Heaven! can I have done any thing to merit this severity? But my complaints are useless: I shall die, dear Rosolie, in your arms; I shall die, and be happy!"

The friends clung still closer to each other, and a pause ensued, which my concern and agitation would not allow me to interrupt.—It was nearly an hour before Bianca could distinctly speak to us again; and then she appeared so enfeebled and exhausted, that we thought it would be more prudent to persuade her to repose herself in bed, than to enter into any distressing conversation; and she was therefore conducted to a chamber by my greatly affected and sympathizing Rosolie.

I knew the gentleness of poor Bianca's disposition, had seen many traits of the goodness of her heart, and repeatedly heard her commended, in tender and ardent terms, by my wife. I was as well acquainted with the opposite qualities of her brother, with his villanies, and want of principle and humanity; it surprised me not, therefore, that he could be proud, cruel, and revengeful to her, though she belonged to the same parents, and had received her infant nutriment at the same breast as himself; and, harbouring scarcely a single doubt but that he were capable of spurning at any thing divine, it seemed to me not improbable that he could break through every thing moral and human.

In the morning the poor refugee was in no degree revived; she was equally, if not more ill than she had been on the preceding night, though her mind was somewhat tranquillized. She did not leave her chamber, but Rosolie attended her in it, and I was admitted to speak to her. She joined our hands, and laying her cold lips on them, prayed that our union might be prosperous and happy.

Oh Bianca! if thy spirit has since been permitted to observe our destiny, surely it has often withdrawn itself to Heaven in sadness and in tears!

When she had raised herself on the couch, she spoke to us again.

"Let not the state in which you, dear friends, now see me, give pain to either of you. To suppress all manner of concern for me I know you are too good, too gentle to be capable of; but moderate your grief, Rosolie: all the world, except you and your husband, regard me as an object too worthless to excite any compassion. Even my brother—God! even my brother thinks me so!—Oh, I have often heard of a broken heart; experience now tells me what it is!"

"It may be amended, dear Signora!" I cried; "it may be amended!"

"Never!" she replied, solemnly, "never! and, by the Victim of thorns, I do not wish it; for I have faith to die upon, and fortitude to bear the breaking of mortality. There have been incautious moments when I have called my brother my murderer: rash I confess it was; but I do believe that he has abridged my life. I was thrown upon his care at an early age; when he was a boy, I had to fear his cruel authority; afterwards, when he had attained the state of manhood, he prevented my union with a brave, a worthy, a lamented man! Years of unkindness followed, and now he loads me with reproaches, with names which shock me, and drives me from his house, as he would an importunate beggar, only for——"

"Only for what?" I enquired, on finding her pause.

"Only for telling him, in terms not ungentle, that he has acted unworthily; that I thought you a man of honour and of good principles, and that I could never cease to love my dear Rosolie, whom he had so much injured and insulted!"

"And he threw you off for that?"

"He did, he did; drove me violently from him; pointed to the door; told me never to approach him again!"

"Oh! you have made me miserable," exclaimed my wife, sinking down by her side. "Have you, dear Bianca, have you suffered abuse and violence for speaking kindly of me, and doing justice to my Roncorone? My heart is full of pain—it bleeds for you, Bianca!"

"Be not concerned on my account," replied the fugitive; "I shall die under your roof, for I came hither on purpose; all thereafter will be happy! God, whom I have never wilfully offended, will amply reward me for my earthly sufferings."

Her injuries pained, but her exemplary resignation charmed me.

"Iniquitous Salvini," I cried, "your soul is burdened with a thousand sins. Cast this brother, dear Signora, for ever from your heart, if it be possible he still retain a place in it; renounce him, and under this roof of your sincere friends, endeavour, by cheerfulness, to re-establish your health and happiness. Rosolie has sufficient cause to love, and I to esteem you; make this your asylum, then, and rely on Providence for your recovery."

"Do, dear Bianca," said my wife; "do, my second mother!"

The scene that ensued was in the highest degree affecting; the sensibility of our new inmate overpowered her; her frame had been too much enfeebled to withstand it, and she again fell beneath the force of her sorrows. Her affliction increased every day; I called medical men to her; they however gave me no assurances of the efficacy of their skill in the present case, but led me to suppose that the malady of the patient had gone beyond remedy.

This daughter of sorrow and of resignation died within a month after her first residence with us; and her end was nearly as serene as her life had been. Death never struck his ensign upon an easier conquest.

* * * * * *

Excellent Bianca! what a farewel to the world was thine! God surely was, in those moments, before thine eyes, smiling thee into fortitude and tranquillity. The wicked can never expect so easy a dissolution; and few even of the pious and resigned are known to have it. It was but as a falling into slumber, a gentle lying down with the hope of again rising. And thou shalt rise! the rewarded spirits of virtue shall guide thee towards Heaven, and welcome thee in it with strains of holy harmony. The lily that springs from the stem which was seared by the sun of autumn, and crushed by the storms of winter, shall not be sweeter or purer in its blossoms than thou shalt be in thy re-animation. Salvini, murderous Salvini! thou wilt never re-animate; or, if thou dost, it will be only to raise thy sick head among the pestilential blasts issuing from the fiends of eternal and unquenchable heat!

The little property that Bianca died possessed of, she bequeathed to Rosolie; it consisted of a small sum of money, a diamond cross, some trinkets and clothes; her blessing was added to the bequest, and she begged Rosolie to keep her in her memory.—Bianca had been loved and respected by all of us; and even the gay Alberti assumed a look of pensiveness when speaking of her dissolution. Salvini, that detestable, base, and unnatural being, was made acquainted with the tenor of her will by Alberti, and the property that had been left to Rosolie, which, at the time of Bianca's death, was at his house in Venice, was immediately conveyed to us by his agent. The departed, a little while before the powers of speech failed, never more to be revived, had desired to be interred at Altino, where the ashes of the man, whom she had once tenderly alluded to, were resting: and indeed her brother, though apprized early of her decease by Alberti, expressed no wish to have the body conveyed to the vault of his family. Rosolie, therefore, erected a simple monument to the memory of the deceased, and I furnished her with an epitaph for it, such an one as was suited to the virtues and humility of the departed mortal.

Rosolie was a sincere and unaffected mourner; the clouds of sorrow at length, however, passed over her brows, and the smiles of serenity and love were seen again.—We were not merely husband and wife; we had association of minds, as well as of bodies; the qualities of our souls were examined, and found to be the same; our ideas corresponded; in the impassioned moments I sought her as my joy; in affliction she was a soother; and had I known distress, I should not have known it alone—I should have had a participating consoler.

God! I worshipped thee more, infinitely more, for giving me such a treasure!

If I had been absent from her a few hours, my return was joyful; if a day, rapturous!—Rosolie would run to meet me, her eyes alone speaking affection; she would rush into my arms, hang upon my neck, nestle in my bosom, lay her panting heart close to mine—closer, still closer—kiss me, and again kiss me—Oh!——

* * * * * *

But I am now coming to an important event —Important?—Horrid! horrid!—Reason, do not forsake me: suffer not the fiend Insanity again to twist her accursed fingers in the fibres of my body, nor to light her consuming fires in my head; if she must be busy once more with me, let her not procrastinate—let her rather entirely root out my brains, and strew them on the earth; let her rather pluck out my heart, and hurl it to the fiercest brutes of these mountains.—Soft, soft, Roncorone, or some churl will scourge thee for bombast!

END OF VOL. I.

THE

Mad Man of the Mountain.

CHAP. I.

MY good and generous friend Alberti had been dangerously wounded by some villains in the streets of Venice, to whom he resolutely refused to give up his money; and his hurts were of such a nature, that it was conjectured death would be the consequence of them. Apprized of his injury, I hastened to him, in order that I might perform the offices of friendship; and, indeed, I found that his piteous situation entitled him to the softest of them, for he had several contusions on his head; and after he had been rescued, part of a broken stiletto was found in his back; his loss of blood had been great, and a fever succeeding, his intellects were deranged, and he knew no one who came near to him.

My pain on seeing him in this state, was excessive; and when I returned home, and spoke of him to Rosolie, she neither could, nor attempted to restrain her tears: we both feared the loss of a most excellent friend and good man, and both execrated the unknown monsters who had so cruelly and privately assaulted him. I attended several days on the unconscious Alberti, returning to Rosolie every evening; but as he grew considerably worse, and it was suggested by the physicians that nature was rapidly failing, I resolved to pass a night with him, thinking that, ere the morning, he would be totally overpowered by death.

Rosolie was somewhat indisposed, but she wished me to be with Alberti, and afterwards, seeing me reluctant on account of her illness, entreated me to go. I kissed her, and calling Lucilla, her maid, cautioned her to take care of her mistress till my return. I then went back again to Venice, and placed myself near the bed of Alberti; nor did I quit my station till the morning, when, to my infinite surprise and joy, the doctors informed me that the fever had very considerably abated, and that there was a probability of the recovery of their patient.

"Then I am happy!" I exclaimed; "I will return to my Rosolie, and inform her of this favourable change. I am sure it will make her joyful; the preservation of so excellent a friend will call forth her gratitude to Heaven."

I felt the pulsations of my heart, which had long been languid, almost instantly increase in their force and activity, and ardently pressed the hands of those who nurtured the hopes which had before been famishing. It was with the greatest speed, and with most sincere pleasure, that I pursued my way towards my habitation. The morning was clear and lovely, like my imagination, which now burst through the vapours that had been collecting around it; the air was enriched by the contributions of flowers and herbs, and I looked into two or three of Rosolie's favourite haunts, in the fond expectation of finding her.

A small group of trees only was now between me and my love, and I peeped through their branches in order to gain a sight of her dwelling. A man, who was known to me, met me on the road;—I had ever judged by his face that he was one of the happiest of mortals; but now the grief that hung on his countenance, and the horrid manner in which he looked at me, made me on the instant withdraw my opinion. He crossed me in my path, and grasped my arm. "Have you not seen," he cried, "have you not seen——"

"What?" I enquired with astonishment.

"Have you not heard of your——"

"Of what?"

"Of your house, Signor?"

"No!"

"Of your wife?"

"Mercy! no, no, no!"

"Not that she is——"

"Dead! speak, speak! dead!"

"Go not forward, Signor," he cried, grasping me at the same time with increased strength, "go not forward!"

"Let me go on!" I exclaimed, almost frenzied; "take your hands from me instantly!"

"Signor, listen to me; proceed no further; the sight will kill you!"

"Sight! God! what sight? Offer to detain me another minute, and the balls that are in this pistol shall be lodged in your head!"

I produced the instrument, and levelling it at him, he crossed the road, when, turning the angle of the grove, I strained my eyes in looking for my habitation, but saw only some blackened ruins: for a moment I shut out the sight. Rousing myself, however, from the lethargy into which I was falling, I ran among the people who were gathered together. "Who perished in the flames?" I cried franticly.

"All who resided in the house," was the answer; "none escaped."

"None escaped?" I said, "none escaped?"

"None, Signor, none."

"None escaped!"

I fell on the earth, and becoming insensible, was for a considerable time unconscious of my miseries and misfortunes.

My senses afterwards returned; I broke from those who strove to detain me, and ran wildly round the ruined fabric, calling on my wife, my Rosolie! But I was not answered; she had perished—had been devoured by the flames! and not a limb or bone of either her or of the two servants could be discovered among the ashes! My brain seemed to be incrusted; I had not power to move my eyes, and my veins felt as if they were isicles. When the spectators first opposed me, my strength was lion-like; but my nerves soon relaxed, and a child might have brought me to the ground. This feebleness also extended to my mind: I was now to be guided, and was unresistingly led away.

* * * * * *

I am convinced that insanity has its blessings; for, during the whole of the month that succeeded the conflagration, I was never more happy; but of the nature of my ideas, of their strength, or of their weakness, I cannot now speak. Reason afterwards gradually approached; I wished not, however, for its return; and in order to destroy the growing stability of my mind, I exerted myself as much as possible, and whirled myself round repeatedly, thinking by such means to make my brain eternally giddy.

I was in one of these half-frenzied moods when my hospitable host (the man who had compassionately borne me from my ruined abode, and since sheltered and protected me) entered the room in which I was;—not regarding him, I continued my extravagant practice till I almost petrified him with fear, and till I fell on the floor, which I stained with my blood; my temples being torn by a nail that projected from a wall, against which I staggered, and the stream that flowed in consequence of it was copious.

"Mother of Christ!" exclaimed Paulo; "do you yet live, Signor?"

I heard his voice, knew perfectly well what he said, and starting on my feet, ran towards him, in order to assure him that I was not only in being, but also sensible of the objects around me; he, however, hurried away from me, pointing at the same time to the door, near to which stood a man almost as lean and pale as death.

"Roncorone!" said the phantom-like figure, "poor, poor Roncorone!"

These were the accents of Alberti, and I knew them to be such. I extended my arms, and ran upon him. In my paroxysms I hugged him with an almost suffocating strain; and the blood that trickled from my wound stained his ashy cheeks, while my tears fell into his bosom, and his eyes were as prodigal as mine.

"To meet thus," said Alberti——

"Is happiness!" I cried. "Come to my heart, friend; it is cold, but your friendship will warm it. Here is my hand; take it as the pledge of a brother's love. We parted in joy——"

"Oh, no, Roncorone!"

"Yes, yes, Alberti, we parted in joy, and in joy we again meet: by these throbbings and internal emotions we do!—and yet, I think our countenances and bodies ought to be, in some degree, actuated by our souls. Why, your cheeks are dreadfully sallow, and your eyes glare on me so strangely, that they look like fragments of the mirror of death!"

"Friend, I have suffered!"

"Aye, and *I* have suffered. Sit—I'll tell you how."

"Forbear, forbear, Roncorone!"

"Sit, listen. Do you not remember that I had a wife? You cannot have forgotten what a kind angel God formed in Heaven for me; she loved you as my friend. You must recollect how beautiful she used to smile upon us when we approached her, and what music came from her tongue when she addressed herself to us. Well, Signor—Nay, nay, sit patiently. It is said that no event happens on earth but what is under the immediate direction of Heaven; my wife, Alberti, while you were suffering in your misfortune, was burnt—her lily flesh incrusted to a cinder, or converted into ashes! Not a vestige of those arms, which have so often enfolded me, was to be found; and those breasts on which I nightly pillowed my head—on which—God! God! why am I left to be the narrator of this tale? Alberti, do you now wonder at these tears? Do you wonder that my wretched bosom swells with sighs, or that I wish to lay down my miserable life, and to step beyond what is now before me?"

"Be calm, my dear friend!" said Alberti, pressing me again to his breast.

"Oh, my wife! my wife!"

"She is happy, Roncorone."

"And I shall soon be happy with her!" I exclaimed. "Alberti, whenever you pass by my grave, whether at morning, noon, or night, let the tears of friendship and of compassion fall upon the sod that covers me."

"May you yet continue many years," said Alberti, "before such a proof of sympathy be required of me!"

"Oh! we are all sorry pilgrims, Alberti, and I of all the most sorry. The prospect of life appears to me as a damp and mouldy picture; the once pleasing objects of which no longer retain their colour, grace, or proportion. My eyes are disgusted; many times do I close them, and wish never to open them more; and when, after successive days of weariness and despair, I lay down my throbbing head, 'Father Eternal!' I exclaim, 'let me now sleep till the world tumbles into chaos, and till the beams of thy glory animate the spirit which thou hast said shall live unfading ages!'"

"Roncorone," cried Alberti, "do not thus agitate yourself; your passions will tear you in pieces. You bleed too; you must be faint; let me apply something to your wound."

I assured him it was only a scratch, not telling him, however, what had occasioned it; and Paulo bringing in some water, I removed the stain from my face. I then again drew near to my friend, and, for a moment forgetting part of my own sorrows, enquired how he had struggled through his recent afflictions. His heart was too noble for querulous complaint; yet the manner in which he replied to me was very affecting. I learned that, after I had left him at Venice, he had, though appearances were previously in some degree favourable, relapsed into pain and distraction, and that few days had elapsed since his physician allowed him to go abroad. His first enquiries had been respecting me, and at Venice he became acquainted with my miseries.

He now exerted all his powers in persuading me to return to the city, but I would not consent to accompany him; I was bound to the place in which I then lived, and could not fly from it.

I wished to die there—to begin my pilgrimage from thence to the regions in which the spirit of Rosolie was then awaiting me, to penetrate and become familiar to those things which God has wrapped in mystery. My soul anxiously strove to burst its bonds; sometimes I thought it actually was forcing its prison gates, and the temporary trances into which my giddy brain was lulled, were, at their commencement, considered as the effects of the approaching oblivion of mortality; but I was both deceived and disappointed by them.

Alberti staid several days with me; he was, however, compelled to go back to Venice; and as I declined going with him, we separated, and all my sorrows, my griefs, and my distractions returned with unabated force. The story of a gossip had now as much effect on me as the precepts of philosophy—even as those which my departed uncle had often dressed in the beauties of language, and which would sometimes for a moment cross my mind.

At the end of a month Alberti was again with me—kind, generous, good Alberti! His heart was tortured for me; and while he threw his arms around me, he entreated me to put aside my despondency, and to trust myself to the guidance of his friendship. I loved him the more for his solicitude, but still refused to comply with his proposal, when he appeared more distressed and mortified, and for several succeeding days he remained silent on the subject. Had my mother given birth to him and to myself at the same hour, I could not have loved him more; and what man should be to man, so was I to him, and he to me.

One evening he had talked me into a seeming tranquillity, and Paulo had furnished him with a bottle of choice wine: I took a glass of it, and Alberti pressed another upon me; a third was afterwards accepted;—the effect it had on me I thought very strange, for I almost on the instant grew drowsy; my head fell upon my breast, and in a few minutes I was in a profound sleep.

When I awoke, I found myself, to my surprise, in an unknown apartment, and on raising my head, saw Alberti gazing on me; I was going to make some immediate enquiries of him, but he threw himself across me on the bed, and entreated me to forgive him.

"But where am I?" I enquired.

"First tell me, dear Roncorone," he replied, "that you will not hate me for what I have done."

"Hate you, Alberti! such are you to me, and so has Nature attached you to my heart, that when I direct such a sentiment towards you, I must contemn myself. But answer me—where am I?"

"In Venice, Roncorone!"

"In Venice! I can scarcely believe it; it seems to me an impossibility. But what, Alberti, have I to do in Venice?"

"To regain a part of that happiness which you have lost, to assume a different habit of life, and to hail the prospects of returning tranquillity."

"Oh, vain and impracticable!" I exclaimed. "But how came I hither?"

"By stratagem," he replied. "I infused an opiate in your wine, and while you remained in a torpid state, effected my purpose— a purpose to which my arguments had been unequal. I am now, Roncorone, at your mercy; dear friend! the love that I bear for you prompted me in this project. With misery have I beheld your late sufferings; with misery have seen the torture of your body, and the distractions of your mind. I imagined them to be partly local;

and being convinced that a change of place could alone avert that fate which was hanging over you, I used the present artifice, and have thus far succeeded; and if you love me, or respect yourself, you will reside for a while under this roof, and suffer me in some degree to influence your conduct."

"Endeavour to make me whatever you please," I replied; "but be not angry if my nature will not bend on every occasion: there may be an obstinacy in it that will not submit to controul; be not impatient, therefore, at my infirmities."

Alberti took me in his arms, assuring me that I was the chief object of his affection and concern, and that my habits of life should not be opposed while I continued to reside with him, unless friendship prompted it. Nature had placed in his breast one of the best of hearts, had stored it with feelings the most lively, passions the most noble, affections the most permanent, and sensibilities the most acute; many times did he cherish me, and many times, like a watchful and eloquent angel, did he check the resolve of self-destruction. He would sometimes induce me to leave my chamber, and to sit with him in the balcony; he afterwards prevailed on me to go on the water, and at length drew me into some of the public walks of the city, though I entered into none of the pleasures of those who frequented them.

One day I met Salvini. The sight of him agitated me exceedingly; and when his eyes encountered mine, the colour of his cheeks faded, and he seemed to stagger as he passed by me. His visible agitation I imputed to a recent cause, and he being dressed in mourning, my suspicion was strengthened.

Alberti saw my distress, and hastened home with me; the little tranquillity that I had regained, was molested; I was prompted to make some enquiries concerning Salvini, and the next morning was informed that he had abruptly left the city, and was gone into the country. His motives for departure I did not enquire into, nor did there appear to me any thing very extraordinary in the circumstance;—I concluded that he was really penitent for his follies and errors; that the horrid fate of my wife hung heavily on his mind; and that my re-appearance, my evident affliction, and my skeleton form, were not, in the moments of contrition, to be regarded by him without extreme pain.

I now began to wish that I had not been drawn from my solitude;—Alberti was acquainted with the nature of my thoughts; and, in order to banish them, he requested me to make an excursion with him, and urged me so much, that at length I agreed to accompany him to Rome. The journey was of singular service to the health of my friend, and I was benefited by it;—we arrived at the Papal dominions without any misadventure; and, on entering the city, limited our continuance in it to a month.

The circle of Alberti's friends in this place was rather narrow, but highly respectable; and to a few of his more sedate acquaintances I was introduced by him. My mind, however, was not long to be diverted; neither time, nor place, nor circumstance could amend it; my looks of serenity were all affected, and my apparent easiness was brought about by hypocrisy. I still despised the shackles of life, still panted for a rapid flight to eternity. Rome to me was as good as Venice; every place was indeed alike, for in every place I was equally unhappy.

Alberti was no longer in the army; his father had been a German, and his mother an Italian; and being attached to the country of the latter, he had passed the greater part of his time in it even before he assumed the military character. His health was now almost perfectly re-established; and having formed several new acquaintances, he expressed a wish to continue some considerable time in Rome:—I agreed still to be with him, and we accordingly engaged a house for a year, and had it prepared for our immediate reception. Still perceiving that I was unwilling to be often abroad, he never opposed my inclination; but his natural vivacity was frequently checked by my gravity, and I had reason to suppose that no man possessed so large a share of his love as he bestowed upon me. We however sometimes made small excursions into the country, and, when at Rome, I was in the habit of endeavouring to sooth my mind with religion.

Neither the history nor the antiquities of this once renowned city were interesting to me;—the time, indeed, had been when I read of the events recorded to have happened in it, with a great degree of pleasure, of delight, and of wonder; when my mind followed the emperors and warriors of remote days through all the various scenes of enterprise and glory, and attended them in their proud prosperities, and also in their deep adversities. The sages of past times had filled me with admiration, while the sons of the lyre sprung the secret mines of sensibility and of ecstacy. But I was no longer susceptible of these feelings; Nature had received a blow from the hand of Apathy, of which she had sickened and mortified.

The amphitheatres, the temples of the Gods! What to me? Columns rose, and surprised me not; ruins nodded, and I felt no awe. My contemplations rested not on the wonders of art, the vestiges of grandeur, or the statues of the Pagan deities; but they were fixed, almost invariably fixed on the frailty of human life, and the instability of man's happiness. I sometimes indeed wandered out alone, pain warping my heart, and misery hanging over my mind; chusing the evening hour, I frequently strolled into the suburbs, and found myself among pillars and arches, halls damp and desolate, and recesses in which murder had secretly prowled. Still my own misery occupied my thoughts; and as I reclined my sallow cheek against the cold marble, I made echo each moment speak the name of my dear lamented wife.

My soul at these times would sicken, and I have been near fainting in the solitude; when I recovered little strength, however, I went again to my home, to a bed in which there was no repose. Ah! why did I so? why did I not force my half-inclined heart to burst asunder at once, and lay me down amongst the rubbish, and die neglected and unknown?

I might have crept into one of the small and narrow cavities; respiration would soon have ceased, and I should have made myself a secret grave, which the eye of man probably would not have peeped into till I had become bloated, corrupted, and defaced; nay, perhaps not till I had wholly been converted into a whitened skeleton.

There might, in that case, have been food for the antiquaries—ha! ha!—"It is, in truth, the body of Cæsar, Sir! I have not a single doubt but that is the fact! Wonderful discovery! precious relics of an illustrious hero! Examine the magnitude of each particular bone, how immense, gigantic! I will sell you his scull for a thousand ducats."—"A thousand! it is too much; but I will give you two hundred for it."—"You are my very particular friend, and therefore shall have it at that price; but to such terms from any other person, I assure you, I would not listen a single moment."

Ah, Roncorone! you might have had your pate handled by every virtuoso with the most profound respect. Why did your ambition fall into such an idle slumber?

★ ★ ★ ★ ★ ★

My friend Alberti became attached to a young, amiable, and wealthy woman who resided in Rome, and on her heart he made a very favourable impression; indeed, most women must have loved him, for he was as sweet in his disposition, as in his countenance; and to his qualities of wit and good-humour were added the more tender ones of humanity and benevolence. He introduced me to his fair companion, and I instantly saw her merit; she appeared to me in every respect a suitable partner for him; there was apparently a similarity in their minds, a conformity in their manners; and it was evident that she had many requisites and recommendations, independent of the beauty of her face, and of the extent of her fortune.

I felt a pleasure, the first I had felt for many preceding months, when I contemplated the happy prospect of Alberti; but ah! when he spoke seriously to me of his premeditated connexion,—when he talked of marriage, and demanded my opinion of it,—whether I would advise him to enter into it immediately, or wait till time should further shew him the character and disposition of the woman,—whether I did not consider the state as most felicitous and happy,—a thousand remembrances rushed in my mind, and I was obliged to retire from him, being overcome by grief, without speaking. I returned to him again, however, in the course of a few minutes, with the resolution of being firm, when he gently pressed me to his heart, and entreated me to forgive him for the pain that he had so inadvertently occasioned me.

"My feebleness is gone over," I replied, "and I am strong again, at least sufficiently strong to talk with my dear friend Alberti. The state of marriage, that we were preparing to speak of:—I had no long experience of what it is, yet——"

"Let us separate, Roncorone," said Alberti; "I will see you again in the evening; or shall we walk together? the day is invitingly fine."

"Ah! I see what your suspicions are; but you are deceived. What! must a man never forget that he has been unfortunate? If such were the general maxim of the world, who would be without a countenance of sorrow? In that case, tears would be as plentiful as the rain of heaven, and the sick sighs of millions would make the air obnoxious, and breed a general plague and pestilence. Alberti! you talk as if philosophy had no precepts. What if they are given in the moments of tranquillity, by him who is unaffected by the ill-chances of life, must we, who are so forcibly preached to, in the hour of actual misery suspect that we have been merely listening to sophisms, or that we have any cause to mourn beyond the hour in which we foolishly suffer our sorrows to commence? Oh fie, Alberti! The stoics, and we have them even in these days, would regard you either as a man of weakness, or of depravity."

"We will talk on this subject hereafter," said my friend; "pray let us walk. It is unusual with you to deal in irony; but when you speak it with wildness, I confess I have many fears for you."

"Fear nothing; the seal of reason is still unbroken, still firmly stamped upon my mind. The state of marriage—Oh how sweet! a good and tender wife—how precious! how excellent! Do the occurrences of the world disturb your temper? Fly to the sympathetic bosom of your partner, and on it she will lull you to a forgetfulness of them. Are misfortunes threatening to assail you? She will tell you not to despair; she will dissipate with her smiles the gloom of despondency, and the damp vapours of imagination. Ah, Alberti! had Heaven but spared *my* wife——"

"Oh! I lament that it did not!"

"But it tore her from me!"

"Talk not of it now, dear friend."

"Cruelly, cruelly tore her from me! her death, how horrid!"

"Forbear, Roncorone! you melt my soul as well as your own."

"Oh how horrid! in the flames she called on me! when she was blistering, she called on me!"

"You will destroy yourself, Roncorone."

"But I was not there, could not meet her outstretched hand! could not alleviate even one of her fierce tortures!"

"In Heaven there are no pains; there all is pleasure; there, at this moment, smiles your angelic wife!"

"True, comforter; you shall be still nearer to my heart for this consolation. Oh! that God would, as a compensation for my many afflictions, tell my spirit to rove with her from this moment eternally among the sweets of his paradise! The period of my life will not, I think, be a long one; the hour of my dissolution, I trust, is not far distant. Speed it, Holy Father! speed it, righteous Comforter of mankind! Alberti, your hand! The woman of your choice is excellent; I have noticed her words, her actions, and placed her among the number of the worthy. Marry her—accept the hand she offers to you; and as there is such an incertitude in the affairs of human life, do not procrastinate your happiness, but attempt to secure it while it seems readily to be obtained. This is my advice; and now I will walk with you, for my mind is again soothed."

Though I gave Alberti this assurance, he regarded me with a melancholy aspect, and his eyes expressed at once the whole language of compassion.

Some few days afterwards he informed me that every necessary arrangement had been made for the nuptials, which were to be celebrated within a week.—"I am glad to hear it," I replied; "within a week, then, dear friend, you and I must part."

"How!" he cried; "part, Roncorone?"

"Yes, Alberti, I will withdraw; whither I have not yet determined; I shall, however, prefer a solitude to a city. If I have only inanimate things, or the beast tenants of a forest to gaze on, my spleen will never be excited; and even should the rustics of the hamlet come to gape at me, while I yet seem a novelty, I shall consider their instinct as harmless, and not chide them for impertinence when I find neither the marks of malice nor of deceit upon the brows of the men, nor the leers of wantonness in the eyes of the women—the general distinctions of the sexes in crowded societies. And yet, dear Alberti, I shall leave you with pain—with pain, which the self-assurance of never seeing you thereafter will, in the moments of my weakness, serve to increase."

"You shall not go from me," said Alberti; "indeed you must not!"

"Pray give me no opposition," I answered, "for what I said was seriously intended; the happiness, or rather the tranquillity of my life depends on it. The air of populous places suits not my constitution; and though I have not much observation to bestow, new manners, new habits and customs perhaps may——no, I cannot flatter myself that they ever will amuse me. Having neither misanthropy in my heart, nor enthusiasm in my mind, I shall be no breeder of corruption; and it is probable that I shall only have time to chuse a little spot of earth for a resting-place for my bones, before the villagers will have occasion to say to each other— "Friends, the stranger is dead; let us pass his body to the grave on the bier, and cover it over with a turf."

"And you *will* leave me, Roncorone? leave me in the happiest moments of my life?"

"Could there have been a better season for my departure," I replied, "since your happiness depends not on me? If it did, I would struggle with my feelings till they tore asunder the strings of my heart, sooner than play the ingrate, and leave you. But as you love me, do not prevent my going; strive not, I beseech you, to impede my intended journey."

"I will not, dear, unhappy friend," he cried. "Grant me, however, one request."

"What is that, Alberti?"

"Go not hence till after my marriage—not till a month afterwards; when that time shall have passed by, I promise to offer no further dissuasion, nor in any manner to check your inclinations. But ah, Roncorone! you must not think that even the possession of my love, her charms, or her smiles will deter my mind from following you and your wretchedness, or still the sighs that will collect in my bosom when I think of and pity your destiny."

"Oh! is there on earth another friend like you?" I exclaimed, rushing into his arms, and melting into tenderness. My emotions silenced me for some time, and I had not power to raise my head from the tender and generous breast on which it had fallen.

"You consent then?" said Alberti, mildly; "you will, for the time I have mentioned, postpone your departure?"

"It would be ingratitude in me," I replied, "not to comply with your request; but as I can never more assume the mask of pleasure, never more admit either joy or merriment into my heart, which grief seems to have hollowed, think not unkindly of me if, when some happier friend shall step forth to congratulate you on your attainment, my tongue shall remain in silence, and my features soften not at your felicity."

The answer of Alberti was in his usual terms of tenderness and affection; but the intention which I had expressed to him seemed to touch him deeply, and I saw that he was internally struggling to conquer very ardent emotions, and to restrain himself from these dissuasions, which he had promised to withhold from me at an after period.

When I retired at night to my chamber, I thought more seriously of my departure than I had done before.—"But whither shall I go?" I said, addressing myself; "to what particular spot shall I direct my steps? Yet is not that a needless question? Is not the world immense, infinite? Has not the hand of God, mysterious Creator! scattered his germs immeasurably wide? The soil, the climate, they are nothing to me; let the one be barren and unfruitful, my appetites will not quarrel with it; and should an unceasing pestilence attend the other, where will be the danger, now my health is irreparably injured? It may, indeed, serve to quicken the slow plagues which are now lazily creeping within me; but I will defy it to produce any original ones. In every nation, in every province, in every desolate isle there is a bed for the most wretched being, for the sorriest outcast, on which he may lay himself down, and sleep away for ever his pain and anxieties;—my wants extend no further; to this they are limited, and *this* is a privilege of which the united malice of the world cannot deprive me."

Before the morning, however, I had brought my mind to make some arrangements, for which I felt somewhat the more tranquil, and, I believe, looked the happier. Alberti married, and, as I had promised, I attended at the espousals, though it occasioned me many a pain, and many an inward struggle. Afflicted as my heart was, I wished not my face to betray my sufferings; but rather strove to hide them under an artificial pleasure, and alternately smiled upon my friend and his blooming bride. He had been present at my marriage, had stood by my side when the priest gave my smiling Rosolie to me:—Oh! how difficult was the task to think on that circumstance, and still wear a placid aspect!

The company that assembled at Alberti's house was not very numerous; many of the bride's relations and friends, however, were there, and the face of every person was animated by pleasure. Alberti's transport was generally visible, but even on that day the pitying sigh of friendship did not fail to pass over the full tide of his joy; it came upon, and almost dissolved me. Blaming myself, however, as the cause of it, I made a still more arduous attempt both to look and talk as if I stood in no need of such exquisite commiseration and sympathy; but, as he had well-studied my manners and habits, I could not fully expect the imposition to pass undetected. His wife was no less attentive to me than himself, and she often turned from the festive party to address herself to me, which she did with a grace and sweetness of tone of which I could not, interested principally in my own concerns as I had been, fail to be sensible.

Pleased was I, however, at the coming of night, and at the departure of such of the company as made my retiring, without an excuse, neither improper nor singular; I hastened to my chamber, and my heart seemed incapable of throwing out its collected sorrows with sufficient speed; I became almost as feeble as I was in childhood, and in that state, some little time afterwards, did Alberti break in upon me.

"You are come to chide me," I said, when I perceived him.

"Oh, no!" he cried, "rather to console, to comfort you."

"Attempt it not; the task would be wholly fruitless. Leave me, dear Alberti, to myself, for my impositions will not stretch any further. Good night—God bless you!"

"Do not let me leave you thus miserable," he said; "return to the company, crush this unavailing sorrow, this destructive anguish!"

"No, no," I replied; "leave me, I again entreat you; concern not yourself for me; sleep and happy dreams I may enjoy before the morning. Go, Alberti; your fair bride is expecting you, for the hour is growing late. Cast not a thought on a forlorn and pining wretch like me; I should be tempted to curse myself if I were to damp one of your joys at such a season as this. Good night! and the felicities of love attend you!"

"Good night! good night!" he exclaimed; "and may the balm

of Heaven be poured into your wounded soul by the swiftest and most benevolent of its ministering spirits."

The two first weeks of the limited month were spent by me with more tranquillity and smoothness of temper than I could have previously expected; and I waited, without any apparent anxiety or impatience, for the passing by of the two which were next to follow. I had even accustomed myself to speak of my removal calmly to Alberti; to discourse collectedly with him concerning the spot which I had chosen for my retreat; and to demand his opinion on some little arrangements which were necessary to be made before I quitted Rome, and all other thick residences of men.

He forgot not the promise he had made to me, though I saw the increase of his concern as the period of our separation advanced; his wife, however, whose mind and heart, if possible, rivalled her sweet and innocent countenance, was under no such restraint, and for a while she importuned me to break my design, and still to continue an inmate with them; but afterwards, I conjectured by his desire, she dropped her entreaties on the subject, and only seemed to lament the necessity of her silence, and to regret the division which was about to take place between me and her truly worthy husband.

Such was the posture of my affairs, and the state of my concerns, when one morning, exactly after a residence of eight months in Rome, in the church of St. Peter * * *

* * * * * *

Yet may it not be rash to touch on that circumstance? May not bad and dangerous effects arise from it? Be it so; still I will on——

——One morning, in the church of St. Peter, my devotions, as well as those of many other persons, were interrupted by the shrieks of a female; I hastily raised my head, and looking towards the spot from whence the noise seemed to come, saw a woman sink on the pavement. A number of people soon gathered around her; I could not get near to her, nor could I see her face; and in a few minutes she was carried out of the church, and the service continued.

Three days after this occurrence, which, being a common one, I had almost forgotten, as I was entering Alberti's house, a woman, whom I had observed some time before, came up to me in a hasty and singular manner; with extreme agitation she delivered to me a letter, and at the same time sighed heavily, and pressed my hand. She held her veil so as every feature was concealed; and having given me the paper, ran from me, and turning down a narrow street, instantly disappeared.

This was strange; I hastened into the house, unfolded the paper, and found that it contained the following warning:—

"Roncorone, beware! misery is in Rome; fly from it—instantly fly from it!"

I was startled for a moment:—the note was evidently from a female hand; but I knew not the characters, nor could imagine to what misery or danger it alluded. My surprise, however, was greater than my alarm. Alberti and his wife were gone into the country for two days, I having declined accompanying them; but thinking the monition idle, on the following morning I went again into the streets, without any serious, or even light apprehension. I walked about a considerable time, and looked shrewdly at many faces; but discovering in none of them the features of an enemy, I returned home again.

I knocked at the door; the stranger was again at my elbow. She thrust another paper into my hand, groaned dreadfully, and vanished before I had time to leave the portico. My astonishment increased; I hurried through the hall, and reaching my chamber, opened this second mysterious scroll. Horrid and dreadful! it said—it said—

"Rosolie lives! but the hour of her dissolution is near; she has seen Roncorone—her beloved, her blessed Roncorone! Holy be the walls of St. Peter for it! Husband, they told me you were dead—they have abused me—God, how abused me! I am innocent—I am innocent! But I am polluted—aye, Roncorone, stained and polluted! Oh my dear husband! I shall never be near you again; my hand shall never touch, my eyes never see you more. Happier would it be if the whole world were placed between us, if unnavigated seas rolled betwixt your virtue and my impurities; I would not have the same wind blow on us, lest, in its passage to you, it should receive a most foul taint from the once chaste partner of your bosom. Oh! the contagion of my body springs up into my brain, and renews my craziness! Husband, if I may now call you by a name that once was tender to me, that in days gone by was sweet to utter,—husband, farewel eternally! If my eyes shall open in the regions of purer light, they will ever be inclining to the lesser world, to watch for the pilgrim spirit of Roncorone. Farewel! but fly from Rome! fly from Rome!"

I sunk on the floor; but my senses did not wholly leave me, though my brain heated quickly. Living! astonishing! beyond every thing astonishing! In Rome! so near to me! Pol—polluted! God of Heaven and of earth! living and polluted! For a moment I strove to regard it as a fiction more monstrous and unnatural than any of those of antiquity; but her own hand, her well-known hand confirmed it a reality.

Polluted!

I grew frenzied, mad as the northern blast, as the billows of the sea it blustered upon—nay, even as a volcano at the moment of its most dreadful explosion. I impiously cursed the Heavens above my head, the earth, every thing that moved on it, every damnable biped that bore the name of man—man! that combination of brutal matter, that heterogeneous monster, which a perverted intercourse of ape and wolf, producing rankness, savageness, and deformity, could not equal.

I did not groan, but I shrieked, and dried my mouth with curses; stupidity, however, afterwards sunk me on the floor, and in that state I continued, till Alberti, who had just returned to Rome, came in, and roused me from my lethargy.

"Who is the villain?" I cried, seizing and grasping him; "who is the villain? I'll stake my life against your's, Alberti, it is that abominable fiend, that son of hell, Salvini!"

My senses again deserted me, and the explanation was partly given to my friend by the horrid scroll that lay at his feet.

* * * * * *

About ten days after this circumstance, and what passed in the interval I know not, I thus addressed Alberti:—"I will find out my wife, and we will again be united. If a score of barbarians have used her, is she the less innocent? She fell not by guilt; she sinned not in the ferment of her passions; she was not lost in the glutinous sea of lust. She shall be near my heart again!"

"Dear Roncorone!" said Alberti, "this may be some stratagem of the designing. Recollect the fire; your wife must be, alas! lost to you for ever!"

"She is not. If it be true that there is a God in Heaven, a man on earth, that there are changes in the seasons, or any qualities in the elements, so true it is that she is living."

"'Tis strange!—very strange!"

"But it is true, fatally true!"

"Dreadful!" exclaimed Alberti, shrinking.

"Horrid! horrid! Oh Alberti! had she been confined in the flames a year before she lost the sense of feeling them, it would not have equalled this. Who is the villain? Who should it be but Salvini? Spare me distraction a little while; let me pluck out the heart of that rank monster, and what I may be thereafter I know not, care not. Alberti, search with me—assist me in discovering the sufferer!"

I broke from him, and ran wildly into the streets;—he followed, and his assiduities alone saved me from destruction; for my actions were those of a mad man, and it was a considerable time before he could draw me again into the house. He had no power to calm me; but, in some degree, he convinced me that no immediate discovery could possibly be made of this mysterious and horrid business, and that precipitation on my part might altogether frustrate my designs. He did not preach patience to me; for his own trembling lips and colourless face shewed me how much he was agitated.

I raved away the night, referring often to the distracted epistle of my wife; and the body of the sun, whose beams were cast on me in the morning, could scarcely bear a greater degree of heat than my brain.

Orders were given to the servants to stop the bearer of any letter that might be addressed to me; and in the afternoon a boy was brought before me, and with him a folded paper, directed by the same hand that had written the first mysterious note, and containing these words:—

"Be merciful, Signor, to one who has sinned, and whose repentance hourly torments her heart. Your wife is bending over the grave, and surely I am not far from it. Signor, I am a guilty wretch, yet do not curse me till you have heard me. Admit me to-morrow morning at eight; if you kill me on the spot, I shall not, even in the moments of death, suffer more pain than I now do, and for a long time past have done. Attempt not to discover me to-night, for your search would end in disappointment. The bearer of this note knows nothing of me, nor will he ever see me more; yet by him, if he be trusty, and observe my directions, I shall learn whether you will to-morrow hear the confessions of a contrite and repentant wretch."

I read, wondered, trembled, almost fainted. The boy told me that a woman, whom he had met in a street, which he named, had given him some money to convey the letter to me; and that she had charged him, if I were at home, to return by the same street, and walk through it with his head uncovered, by which, though she intended to be invisible, she should know whether he had succeeded. The boy spoke with much simplicity; and fearing a discovery impracticable, though my tortured soul prompted me to aim at it, I suffered him to depart, nor attempted to follow him. I however charged him to observe strictly the strange directions of the hidden woman, and enforced them by doubling his reward.

I was waking the whole night; and during some part of it, my frame was so convulsed, that Alberti, who, at different periods, left the apartment of his wife to visit me, thought that Death was seriously commencing his operations on me.

Rosolie was in my soul, in my eye; I saw her pale, withered, dying. How dreadful is the intellectual sight! It then made me groan, and almost drew my eyes out of their sockets. I heard the clock strike eight; Alberti could scarcely hold me. In about five minutes the mysterious woman came trembling into the room; when I ran up to her, seized her by the arm, and tearing off her veil, beheld Lucilla, the woman who had formerly resided with me, and who I thought had perished in the flames with her mistress, and with the man that attended on me.

She shrieked, and fell on the floor, and my own enervated limbs only bore me to the arms of Alberti before they wholly failed me.

It was some considerable time ere the wretch could be persuaded to raise her head; she afterwards, in bursts of agony, horror, and remorse, gave me the following shocking narrative.

Before I had engaged her to wait upon my wife, she and Stephano, my other servant, had entered into an illicit connexion, which was subsequently continued under my roof. Having made her subservient to his purpose, he not only withdrew a promise of marriage, on which she had foolishly relied, but totally reversed his speech, his manners, and conduct, and often treated her with uncommon severity and brutality. Pregnancy was the effect of their cohabitation; the family of the girl being respectable, and dreading the resentment and shame that would fall on her, she endeavoured to make him what he formerly appeared, and professed to be, and also renewed her entreaties; but was again inhumanly repulsed. For several days the villain's savage temper was displayed on every occasion, and blows often succeeded the curses which he heaped, without measure, upon his astonished victim, who confessed to me that she had become such by the impulse of a real affection.

It was the cause of much surprise, and also of equal pleasure, when she afterwards discovered in him a great degree of kindness, and heard him talk distantly of making her the reparation she had demanded; but that, he informed her, must be on conditions which he would soon make known to her. He assured her that her own conduct must determine whether the union should take place immediately, or be for ever put aside; and having drawn from the anxious girl an assurance that she would be guided by him in every circumstance, if he would avert her impending infamy, and the curses of an honest and reputable father, the diabolical villain one evening, when I and Rosolie were from home, began his projects, of which she had no conception or intimation, and hurried her to a place some distance from the house, where, to her astonishment, she beheld Signor Salvini, who seemed to have been impatiently waiting for their arrival.

She now began to fear that some horrible designs were forming; and her conjecture was right, for she was desired to become an agent in the perpetration of them: and hoping to make her willingly such, Salvini forced upon her a large sum of money. It was now too late to retract; a savage resolution was fixed on the brow of Stephano, who cautioned her with his finger, while he assured Salvini that any project he might form, should be entered into at whatever time he directed, or thought most proper.

After this they had several meetings, all equally private, and tending to the ruin of me and Rosolie; and the gold of Salvini most plentifully fed the avarice of Stephano. The plot for burning of my house, and carrying off my wife, was now planned and debated on. Lucilla, horror-stricken, refused to become an accessary; but Stephano swore if she did not consent to it, she should not live to give birth to her child. Salvini, having endeavoured, with fiendlike cunning, to laugh away her scruples of conscience, proposed an oath in order to bind her, when he found his diabolical irony had no effect on her. Stephano's eyes expressed at a single glance the state of his savage soul; and dreading his malice and cruelty, she swore to aid them in their designs.

I trembled while, with evident anguish, the girl continued to inform me that—

After this meeting, Stephano seldom suffered her to be out of his sight; and if at any time she attempted to argue with him, or seemed to shrink from the vow of compulsion, it only drew from him horrid threats and brutal language.

He one evening said to her, "This is the night of our experiment; the Signor is from home; he is gone to Venice to see Signor Alberti, who has had an ugly cut in the dark, which is a circumstance that highly favours our plot. Mind how you conduct yourself; follow my directions in every thing, and our reward will be a golden one." She was running from him with terror; but perceiving that her design was to fly to her mistress, he threw her on the floor, and dragged her back again. Her fear, and the state in which she then unhappily was, made her submissive; she entreated him to do her no injury, and he released her, but upon the condition of her not placing herself in the way of her Lady, and also on her promise of accompanying him and Salvini without noise or resistance.

She attended her mistress to her chamber about eleven o'clock; but, in order to keep her from prating, Stephano, after my wife had entered the apartment, placed himself at the door, with an unsheathed stiletto in his hand, of which circumstance he had previously acquainted the wretched girl. Rosolie soon dismissed Lucilla, who afterwards went down the stairs with the awaiting Stephano, and in the course of a few minutes Salvini was silently, and with great caution, admitted into the house. Above half an hour was spent by these hellish contrivers in secret talk, when the former went up stairs, and returning almost immediately, assured Salvini that the work was done.

The petrified Lucilla, not at that instant recollecting the plot that had been recently hinted to her, thought that these ambiguous words of her seducer probably alluded to the murder of her mistress; but after a few minutes of silent suspense, she heard a crackling noise, and saw that some part of the building was on fire, when Salvini seized her by the arm, and hurried her to a carriage at some distance from the house, while his accessary ran up to the chambers.

Lucilla waited not long before he came to her, bearing Rosolie totally senseless. Detesting him now as much as she had once loved him, she called him a villain and a murderer, and attempted to shriek for assistance; but both he and Salvini prevented her by means insufferably severe, which almost brought suffocation upon her.

When Rosolie recovered from her swoon, shrinking and with terror, she asked where she was, the carriage being darkened so as to keep out the moon-beams. To her question Stephano replied that he was taking her to the Signor; but Salvini remained silent, and Lucilla was scarcely allowed to utter a single word. Stephano informed his mistress that it was not probable any part of the building could withstand the flames; and that, as there were no houses near to it, no assistance could be expected. He added, that he had thought it most proper to convey her from the danger as speedily as possible, and that he had taken the precaution of dispatching a messenger to the Signor at Venice, to apprize him cautiously of the accident, and prepare him to receive her without any excessive alarm or astonishment on her arrival.

This part of the villain's artifice was managed with sufficient skill, and drew forth the thanks and acknowledgments of my betrayed and unsuspecting wife.

They had travelled nearly an hour when the coach stopped, and

Salvini got out of it; the day was but just breaking, and he was muffled up so as to prevent Rosolie making any discovery of his person as he quitted the vehicle. Had she enquired who he was, Stephano was doubtless prepared with an answer; but she was too much agitated to notice particularly what seemed of but little importance.

Stephano descended with Salvini, on the pretence of being called by the driver to assist in disentangling some part of the harness; but he first spoke some few words to Lucilla, which, though inexplicable to Rosolie, were fully understood by the person to whom they were addressed. The almost stupified girl therefore sat silent and motionless; Stephano, however, returned almost instantly, unaccompanied, and springing into the carriage (the freedom of which action he hypocritically hoped his Lady would pardon), he ordered the driver, a wretch trained into villany by Salvini, to go forward.

They had proceeded but a little further, when a man rode up to the door, and having enquired the names of the travellers, informed Rosolie that Signor Roncorone had dispatched him to say that he had left Venice on a very urgent occasion, relating to the affairs of Signor Alberti, who had died within the last six hours, which he would explain to her at their meeting; and that he had sent a carriage and a lady of his acquaintance to take her to the place where he should be anxiously expecting her.

Gross as the improbability was, it did not strike Rosolie; too greatly agitated to combine circumstances, and calculate time, she left the coach that had brought her from her burning house, and desired Lucilla to go with her. The girl now uttered a piercing shriek; for she saw her Lady seized rudely by the ruffian who had told the abominable lie, and hurried away by him. Stephano, enraged by her conduct, savagely struck her on the forehead, and in a threatening manner drew his cold dagger across her throat; nor did she see her mistress for the course of three weeks after this period, when she found her at Rome, almost frenzied, guarded by Stephano, and—and—defiled by Salvini!

* * * * * *

Oh! this task is too much! too horrid!

* * * * * *

Ye hours, how unheeded have you passed! ye seasons, I am almost unconscious of your change! The breezes of Spring may have blown sweetly over the heads of the mountains; Summer may have clothed the earth with flowers more bright and luxuriant than those of her departed sister; under the sunny smiles of Autumn the fruit of the vineyards ripened into delicious perfection; and lo! now over the summit of every precipice, Winter wrathfully whirls his immense forces of hail and snow, and unchains all his soul and turbulent spirits, and gives them to the elements!

To thy cell, Roncorone—to thy cell for a little while,—then to thy cold damp grave for ever! That circumscribed domain, in which man can display neither his consequence nor insignificance, —where nothing is dependant on him, and where, though he may have been a sceptred tyrant, the scourge, the dread of millions— the sorriest reptile shall assert its superiority over him. The mortal, when reflecting on this state, and knowing it to be inevitable, generally feels a sensation, as if the cold worms had begun to twine around the veins of his body, though the spirit be still the tenant of it. No such emotions, however, trouble me; I shrink not at the prospect, see no gloom hanging over it; but if Death were to send one of his mysterious harbingers to me, the monster, hideous and frightful as he might appear, should not find me loath to be led by him to the world of shadows. We sojourn not long in that dark country; we go through it into regions exquisitely bright, there to reside, as we are told—assurance too sweet for either doubt or disbelief!—for——

Wife of my soul! the period of our re-union is at hand; descend—come down to me, for under thy guidance my flight to Heaven will be more rapturous. Alberti, I would thy friendly hand could lay me in the earth! Yet why, dear, generous man, should I wish to give another pang to thee? No, no! it will be better to die unknown and unregretted.

The panegyrics bestowed on departed Princes are often known to be undeserved; on the tombs of Nobles the sculptor may place his expressive statues, and cut the characters of the inflated epitaph, that tells a lie to every one who passes near to it. It is the consecrated grave of the peasant on which my eye rests with a serene pleasure;—his virtues are recorded only in the memories of his few simple friends; his widow directs the defending briar; his children's little hands root up every weed; the finger of the honest man points towards the turf—the mansion of a sleeping brother; and the affectionate swain, as he bends over it, gives a voluntary tear to him who has sighed for thousands. Pride! I want not thy honours and trophies. Humility! may my sleep be as tranquil as thine, and my hour of waking as glorious! But I shall have no widow to direct the defending briar, no little children to root the weeds from my grave!

The head-ache, the heart-ache are subsiding. After this long pause, and on the continuance of Lucilla's information, I proceed:—

Salvini soon after quitted Rome, as the violence he had done to Rosolie had distracted her; she raved franticly for her husband, and constantly endeavoured to make herself mistress of some instrument of destruction. The sight of Stephano was evidently horrid to her; a considerable time elapsed before she would allow even Lucilla to come near to her; and it was two months before that wretched girl was permitted to extenuate her seeming guilt by a relation of melancholy facts and incidents which concerned the conspiracy. This information, however, was not at that time perfectly understood; for Rosolie, at some periods, possessed a faint remembrance only of what was past, and she would earnestly talk of returning to her husband; but her health, as well as her mind, were rapidly decaying, and Lucilla saw that she was stepping towards the grave.

The girl assured me that she frequently expostulated with the brutal Stephano; but the accumulating gold of Salvini made him every day more and more a villain. Roused at length by the cruelty of the monster, Lucilla was thrown into so violent a passion, that a premature labour succeeded, and the fruit of her detested intercourse came into the world unperfected.

It was nearly a month before she again saw her wretched mistress, whom she found almost in the state of non-existence. The house that Salvini had placed them in was small and private; but it was his intention soon to remove them to some place still more retired. Stephano was sensual and luxurious; hating Lucilla now for what he called her affected humanity, he brought into the house a young prostitute, and openly cohabited with her, while the wine furnished by Salvini kept him in a state of almost continual intoxication. He bestowed the grossest names upon my sacrificed wife; and while he laughed at her fits and distractions, which he believed to be artifices, he censured Salvini for not returning to enjoy again what he had first, at much expence and trouble, made himself master of.—Fiend! devil!

The repentant Lucilla had yet a faint hope that her mistress would survive. To escape, guarded as she was, she knew to be impossible; but, in order to obtain some small comfort for her Lady, she again attempted to sooth the brute, and again took him into her arms, even when she wished a dagger in his breast.

Having endeavoured to divert the moody chimeras of Rosolie, which were akin to insanity, and also to teach or bring back some degree of fortitude to a mind that was sometimes depressed by stupidity, and at other times torn by frenzy, she prevailed on Stephano to let them go abroad for a few hours; and three times afterwards had she induced him to accompany them to the church of St. Peter.

It was on their last visit to that place that Rosolie discovered me;—I was observed by neither Lucilla nor Stephano; and as my wife did not speak till after she was carried home, and left to the care of her distressed companion, the hell-hound of Salvini knew nothing of the discovery, nor in any wise troubled himself concerning the fainting of his prisoner.

Rosolie knew she was not deceiving herself in respect to my appearance, the reality of which was not doubted by her; it created a fixed and frightful horror, and she spoke of it to Lucilla with a solemnity so dreadful, and with such a motionless countenance, that the girl was terrified by looking upon and hearing her. Rosolie requested her to write the note which had first excited my wonder, and, if possible, to convey it to me; but Lucilla was conscious of the difficulty of performing the task, even admitting that I was in

Rome, and she knew that it must be attempted by stratagem, in which there would be considerable peril.

The chamber in which they resided, or rather in which they were confined, was at the back of the house, and the window belonging to it near the premises of another person; in the adjoining yard they had daily seen a woman walking, and as she appeared too humble to be the owner of the house, Lucilla concluded that she was only put in the possession of it during the absence of her employers. The eyes of this person had often met those of the prisoners, who, through fear, had never spoken to her; and Lucilla, struck by the peculiar, inquisitive, and apparently anxious manner of her regard, thought it possible that she would be inclined to serve them, if they were, in proper terms, to require her assistance. She therefore wrote a short note to her, entreating, in an affecting manner, that she would enquire at the hotels and other places where it was likely to obtain intelligence whether Signor Roncorone were at Rome, and if he were, in what part of the city he resided.

She informed the woman that this request came from victims of cruelty and oppression, but earnestly begged her to observe secrecy, and not to speak to the Signor if she should discover him. Inclosing a piece of money, she waited anxiously for the appearance of the stranger, on whose approach she threw it over the wall, and trembled while the receiver was taking it from the ground. The woman unfolded the paper, perused it earnestly, looked compassionately at the supplicating and agitated prisoners, and, by her gestures, led them to suppose that she would willingly endeavour to befriend them.

Lucilla felt a degree of comfort, and talked of their deliverance by me; the horror of Rosolie, however, increased, and she solemnly vowed never to see me more; but she feared that I might be discovered, and murdered either by Salvini or Stephano. This idea now principally occupied her mind; in consequence of which, her words were wild and extravagant, and she was terrified by the most trifling noise.

Lucilla, whom her mistress, in her most composed moments, had forgiven, having prevailed on her to lie down, went to play the hypocrite before Stephano, in order that she might induce him to abate his severity. Knowing his avarice to be great, she carried with her a diamond cross of considerable value, which she persuaded him she had purloined from her mistress, who, she added, significantly, could have no further occasion for it.

Stephano received it with pleasure; he saw not through the artifice of Lucilla, but caressed her repeatedly; at the same time he commended her change of sentiments, vowed to discard the wanton he had taken into the house, informed her that he expected Salvini in Rome in the course of a fortnight, when he hoped circumstances would become more favourable in the eyes of his Lady, whose unhappiness he conceived to be self-imposed; and again, as he had many times before, solemnly swore that his late master had long become insensible of the departure of his wife, he having died in Venice of a fever, supposed to be brought upon him by his attendance on Signor Alberti.

Lucilla did not dare either to contradict or oppose the despicable liar, well knowing the rashness and ferocity of his temper; on the contrary, she seemed to accord to all he said, but hinted that she thought the health of her mistress was very bad. She proceeded to tell him that medical assistance was absolutely necessary, and requested him to let her go out on the following day to purchase some medicines, which, she added, might be administered by her without the intrusion of a physician.

This, however, Stephano hastily refused, dropping at the same time some doubts respecting her sincerity; when assuming an air of assurance, she replied, if she were suspected, she should regard her own interest only, and snatching up the diamonds which she had placed upon a table, was preparing to leave the room; but Stephano detained her, and fawningly drawing her towards him, begged her not to be so warm and impetuous. Lucilla now, for the first time, saw her power, and endeavoured to increase it; what humanity could not accomplish, she found the gift of any thing that was valuable would be fully adequate to; and also that pride and courage aided her project better than fear and abjectness, which she, on the instant, resolved to put aside, and to talk to him with the spirit of an offended and irritated woman.

It was with satisfaction that she perceived this conduct on her part was likely to produce the consequences she had wished for.

Stephano's penetration was considerably less than his villany; he believed that the girl was actually now as depraved as he had been long endeavouring to make her; he promised her she should go out on the following day as she had desired; and urged her to take more valuables from the casket of her mistress, which had been snatched up by her when she found her house on fire, and afterwards brought to Rome, and forgotten. Lucilla promised to do this whenever a favourable opportunity should present itself, but warned him at no time thereafter to place his doubts and suspicions on her.

She then returned to the chamber of Rosolie, who had fallen into an uneasy sleep, in which, however, she continued some considerable time. At length she started from a terrifying dream; but Lucilla called her to a sense of her situation, and leading her to the window, they both sat down, and soon after saw their unknown friend in the adjoining garden, holding up a folded paper.

Rosolie instantly fell back in her chair, and Lucilla screamed as she threw up the sash. The woman had put the note on the end of a long osier, and mounting a garden ladder, she extended her arm, and Lucilla received the billet. This being performed, the stranger kissed her hand, and retired, and Lucilla unfolded the little packet, which was formed of the money that had accompanied her written entreaties, and of a paper which informed them that, after a long enquiry, she had discovered Signor Roncorone, as well as a gentleman, his friend, of the name of Alberti, was living in Rome. She particularly described the place in which they resided, but declined all pecuniary acknowledgment, and assured them that if she had the ability of doing them any further service, and they could contrive to make their wants known, inclination would not be wanting in her.

My poor Rosolie was troubled with hysterical emotions while she listened to Lucilla, who informed her of her project of delivering, if possible, the note to me on the following day. The girl entreated her mistress to let her make a full disclosure of circumstances; but seeing the dreadful effects of her proposal, she forbore to speak of it again.

The next day Lucilla availed herself of Stephano's promise; and having bought a few drugs of a chemist, she enquired her way to the house occupied by me and my friend, when, following her directions, she met me in the street, and pursuing me to my home, delivered the billet as I have mentioned before.

Stephano was a great epicure: Lucilla, knowing this to be his character, made some purchases for his palate; and laying them before him on her return, again won his regard, and caused him to renew his former protestations, to which she seemed to listen with approbation.

Her mistress, who was waiting with impatience, heard her information with terror; and before the approach of night, her illness had increased most alarmingly. She was continually repeating an anxious wish that I would leave Rome; her next desire was to die; and the consciousness of the rapid decay of her faculties formed the most soothing of her reflections. She persuaded Lucilla to conceal her extreme indisposition from the fiend Stephano, whose very name was dreadful to her, and whose sight she could not for the space of a moment endure; and also to deliver a second note to me, if it were practicable, in case I should not have left the city. The questions which she asked the girl respecting me and my appearance were shocking in their consequences; and the account that was given to her of my languor and evident affliction caused her to speak in terms more strange and melancholy than she had ever used before.

With her late accustomed dissimulation, and another valuable having previously been placed in the greedy hand of Stephano, Lucilla accomplished the last-formed project; but her hypocrisy afterwards grew more feeble, and she watched the increasing faintness and frequent distortions of the face of her mistress, who still conjured her to be silent, and to let death come on her without apprizing Stephano of it;—but after many sick and painful ruminations, and finding that I still remained in Rome, and also that she was most certainly now stepping into eternity, she altered her original intention, and, after many efforts, wrote that horrid note which informed me of her existence and miseries. Still she was determined on concealing herself from my eyes, and would not attend to the solicitations for discovery made by Lucilla, who, though opposed, resolved to place each occurrence within my knowledge;—she dreaded the event of it, but having formed the scheme, rested not till she had carried it into execution.

In this circumstance, however, she unfortunately excited the suspicions of Stephano;—her unusual absence, and her visible agitation on her return, she could no longer hypocritically account for, when, fearing that she had been plotting abroad, he commanded her to retire to her mistress's room, and vowed that she should leave it no more. His brutality, which had for several preceding days been inactive, now seemed to be bursting forth with redoubled violence. Though her rage was internally swelling, she knew that to vent it at this time would be premature; she therefore only requested him to send a medical man to her Lady, who, she believed, was dying, and then withdrew as he had desired her.

Stephano looked shrewdly at her as she left him, and stopped her for a moment to gaze earnestly in her face; but he could not much alter her countenance, as her confidence happily revived under his scrutiny, though it totally failed as soon as she turned from him towards the prison-room of her expiring mistress. Stephano, believing that Rosolie was indeed in the state of danger that had been mentioned to him, sent immediately for a physician, whom he brought before my almost insensible wife.

* * * * * *

By the language of the Doctor, it was evident that Stephano, in order to cover his villany, and effect his deceit, had persuaded him the patient was mentally deranged. The senses of Rosolie, indeed, were not at that time very perfect, which served to establish this information; and Lucilla had not, when she looked at the menacing eyes of her betrayer, sufficient courage to attempt to controvert the opinion which had been formed of the intellectual state of her mistress. At length the Doctor and Stephano withdrew; in the evening some medicines were administered to Rosolie, and an old woman was sent as an assistant to Lucilla, who was almost distracted between the anguish which she felt for her dying Lady, and the despair that arose from being deprived of attending me as she had appointed.

Rosolie passed a dreadful night, but in the morning sunk into a slumber. Stephano, who was actually now alarmed, had been many times to make enquiries, which he did with some appearance of concern, if not of remorse; and he did not retire to his bed till six o'clock, previous to which he had dispatched a messenger to Salvini.

Lucilla, on finding her gaoler asleep, ventured into the lower apartments, which, to her grief and vexation, she found all secured; but, returning to the chamber, she saw the stranger in the adjoining garden, when the hope of escaping again strengthened; and having attracted the notice of the woman, she motioned her to put one of the little ladders over the wall. This was accordingly done, the desire having been perfectly and immediately understood. My Rosolie was still sleeping, apparently to rise no more from her slumbers; the faculties of the fatigued nurse were also dormant, and they seemed not easily to be called into action.

Another moment, and Lucilla thought it would be too late for any enterprise; she therefore dropped from the window, and descended to the ground with little injury; she immediately mounted to the top of the ladder, and drew it after her into the garden of her unknown friend, whom she most cordially thanked for her humane assistance. Having been conducted to the street, she hastened towards my house, where she rapidly ran through the foregoing story, and begged me to fly with her to my dying wife.

* * * * * *

Oh God! what had been my misdeeds, what my crimes? that such miseries, such horrors fell on me? Was it, Father, retribution? No! I have too great a sense of thy goodness, of thy mercy, and of thy supremacy to suppose that thou wert the director of these events, and most unnatural occurrences,—let the schoolmen, in the intricacies and mazes of their reasonings, say what they will to the contrary. I have adored thee often in edifices raised by the hands of man, but more often in the temple of the world, which neither art nor industry can limit; which is canopied by thy own Heavens, and which thy own sun by day, and thy mysterious host of stars by night beautify beyond what every mine on earth can

furnish, infinitely beyond the poor devices of imitating and presumptuous man! There have I adored thee; there in wonder, in
amazement, and delight, have contemplated thy creation, and
most truly reverenced thee. But I had not done this, neither could
I thus have borne myself, if I had beheld thee as the scourger of
innocence, or as one who, for purposes unrevealed, knew of and
suffered the dreadful deeds wrought by the bloody hands of man,
or those which have been done towards me, to the annihilation of
health, of peace, of reason—deeds horrible in sound as the most
tremendous thunder! more fatal in effect than bursting clouds of
burning matter!

* * * * * *

I seized the hand of Lucilla, and hurrying her away, desired that
she would be swift in conducting me to my wife. The penitent girl
obeyed; I rushed wildly through the streets with her, and Alberti
followed us. Arrived at the house, Lucilla knocked gently at the
door, and it was opened by the hellish Stephano, who fled from
me, astonished and shrieking, through the passage; but I pursued
him, and seizing him by the throat, grasped him till he foamed,
till his face became as black and ugly as any of the devils, when he
reeled insensibly, and fell on the floor.

Assigning him to the care of Alberti, I followed Lucilla to the
chamber of my wife; I ran up to the bed, threw myself upon it,
saw my Rosolie, pale, senseless, dying! I clasped her hand, but it
did not return the pressure; I called her by her name; she neither
answered nor noticed me. No! Death was on her—his power oper-
ated, and all——

But why this method, Roncorone? why should thy mind strive
to assume a fortitude, when there is a perverse power within it,
whose cessation from despotism is but of a momentary date—a
period, in order to acquire additional strength, which is meant to
effect a perfect triumph?

I did not leave the room all the day; I watched the sufferer every
moment of the night, and at the break of morning she died—she
died!

Salvini, I will bring you to an account for this, and to such an account as shall not admit prevarication. I will anticipate the retribution of Heaven; I will search your heart, but not with words; a confession shall be drawn from you, not by judicial means, but by the force of my own interrogatories. I will do it, villain, barbarian, murderer! by the soul of my wife, whose body lies at this moment stiffening before me, I will do it! In the prolonged agonies of death, when you shall coldly sweat, and writhe, and groan— then, then shall be my triumph! You shall die, Salvini! you shall descend, and the eye of intellect shall follow your soul and reluctant spirit through the noisy vaults and gleaming passages of hell, nor close till you are pushed from the farthest margin; no, not till it has seen you descending, headlong and scorched, through fathoms of smoke, in which the red flames of the soul-receiving cauldron beneath shall make you partially visible.

This was my oath.——

——I made it whilst I stood over the body of my murdered wife, whilst there was warmth in her still quivering flesh; I made it with a vigour beyond nature, and was carried out of the room by Alberti, who had on that morning caused Stephano to be assigned over to the officers of justice, from whom, however, he escaped, though I suspected it was money, and not cunning, that effected his enlargement.

The state of my mind, as well as of my heart, was too desperate to give an exact and methodical description of. Again my brain became the receptacle of most foul and tormenting images; and Rosolie, sweet lily early blasted! being laid in the earth, I prepared myself for vengeance.

I provided Lucilla with a sum of money to enable her to return to her friends, if, after her disgrace, they were willing to receive her; but the girl's heart was almost broken, and all the felicities of her life had fled, never to be recalled. Health and peace had forgotten her, and sickness, grief, and contrition were ever near her; but her complaints to them were not many, because conscience was ever telling her that her own guilt had first conjured them up, and solely influenced them in their designs and machinations. Nearly a thousand times, with a deathlike countenance, and with lean imploring hands, did she call on me for forgiveness; there had been error in her conduct rather than crime, and her appearance shewed the severity of the punishment that had already been inflicted on her. I therefore trampled her no lower, but raised and pardoned her; telling her to refer her sins, with humility, to the judgment of her God, and also to look for mercy in him.

I then clandestinely quitted Rome; having previously written a letter, similar to the following, to my best worldly friend, from whom I contrived to have it kept till I should be at some considerable distance.

"Forgive me, Alberti, and entreat your wife also to forgive me, for my sudden disappearance. The womb of my mother never harboured you, nor were you in infancy lulled in my cradle; still you have been, and now are my brother. Fraternity like your's was never excelled from the days when the waters of destruction subsided, till the hour in which I said, secretly, 'Farewel, dear partner! God guard your steps, however deviating be mine! Farewel, dear partner! best and most truly loved associate! we shall never meet again!"

We never did meet again.

The disappearance of Stephano made me almost mad; I entreated Alberti, in another paper which I left behind me, to offer immediate and large rewards for his apprehension; but the villain was too successful in his enterprise, and I never more heard of him. My principal fear was that he would be with Salvini, and that from him my intended victim would learn his danger before I could bring it near to him. The idea gave me strength; I hastened towards Venice, and my efforts were so great, that nature almost sunk beneath them. My body was exhausted, my mind distracted; an hundred times in an hour I called on Rosolie. In the morning I fancied that I saw her coming with blooming cheeks to meet me; at noon she was beside me, smiling on, embracing me; and at evening I beheld her, white and dejected, pacing solemnly under the gloom of every clump or row of trees near which I passed.

So much was I the slave of a wild imagination, and such were my horrors, such my ideas and chimeras till I arrived at Venice. That place was the theatre of action; my sinews were braced, my heart steeled; the hand of desperation seemed to take the guidance

of me, and the spirit of my wife to cry from the temples of religion, from the regions of air, and from the waves of the Adriatic,
"Vengeance! vengeance!"

In going to the house of Salvini, which I did almost as soon
as I entered the city, I had to pass the place in which the remains
of my uncle rested; the doors of the church being open, I went
into it, sought the aisle in which I had erected his monument, and
kissed the tablet that recorded some few of his modest virtues.
Reverence, however, could not long detain me; I returned through
the ranks of those who were devotionally employed; and seeing
that I attracted the particular notice of many of them, who rose
from their knees to gaze on me, I folded my arms, and laying my
agitated face upon them, in that manner passed the doors, and
again entered into the street, which being greatly crowded, the
concerns of the busy people allowed them no time to trouble
themselves, or enquire into mine.

In a few minutes afterwards I was at Salvini's house: I knocked
at the door, and a servant appearing, I enquired for his master; but
learned from him that my enemy was not at Venice, though the
lacquey pretended ignorance as to the place of his residence. From
one of Alberti's Venetian friends, however, I learned that Salvini
was at Mantua, to which place it was my intention to follow him
immediately.

I remained only one day in Venice. Keeping myself as private
as possible, I was not noticed by many, and to those few who rec-
ognized and addressed me, I did not make known the sorrows of
my heart, or the distractions of my mind; neither did I ask for
their pity, nor correct the erroneous information that had been
given them of my unhappy story. I no longer looked for sympathy, because I was no longer weak; I had no tears in my eyes, no
sickness in my heart; the active spirits of revenge hurried me on,
and the rapidity of my pulses was almost incredible. To speak still
more forcibly, my state might be compared to that of a lion, which,
having been attacked by an enemy, goes forth with his chest full of
ire, and with menacing eyes, to seek for the blood which can alone
appease him.

With the same speed that I had travelled from Rome to Venice,
I continued my pursuit from the latter place to Mantua; but after

my fatigue, my vexations, and my pains, I had to learn that I arrived a day too late for the completion of my purpose, as the execrable Salvini had departed on the preceding one from Mantua.

This was a blow of which at first I was greatly susceptible; for I began to fear that the fiend would elude my vengeance, and also that Stephano had exceeded me in swiftness, and caused the removal of his employer. Still my disappointment did not wholly discourage me; but learning nothing of Salvini's departure that was satisfactory, I apprehended that I should not soon meet with him. My strict enquiries brought me intelligence that he had been visiting a Nobleman, whose name I have now forgotten, and that his disappearance was abrupt: all beyond this was mysterious.

Two days afterwards, however, aided by dissimulation, I learned from a servant of Salvini's host, that post-horses had been procured to carry him towards Milan; and that he had, some few hours previous to the commencement of his journey, received letters which seemed greatly to agitate him.

"He has not escaped then!" I exclaimed; "my snare is yet open, and I still shall take him in it."—I clapped some money into my director's hand, and in less than an hour was leaving Mantua behind me; the tumult of my heart affected my breath, and on receiving the intelligence of this man, my emotions almost entirely suppressed it.

I paid my drivers liberally, and urged them on with increasing impatience; my soul seemed to fly before me; at every post, not thinking of expences, I selected the best horses, and the night as well as the day were spent in travelling. It was dark when I entered Milan; and in the morning I again began my search, when an hundred additional troubles and perplexities arose; but I surmounted them, dispersed, put them all to flight, completely conquered them.

If a man would succeed in a project, let him persevere; if he would gain the assistance of his brethren, let him scatter his gold among them. Those who are urged to do an act of service, for which friendship and gratitude are to be the mere rewards, will shake their heads, and answer, "We have no power;" but feed their venality, and it will be, "Good Signor, command us."

I had been a week in Milan, and made no discovery; on the

eighth day, however, as I was passing a public market, I saw a man purchasing some poultry, and his face was not unknown to me: I knew him to be, or that he had been, a servant to Salvini. After a moment's recollection, I was assured that he was one of the two fellows that had accompanied my detestable enemy to his house, from which I had rescued my Rosolie—rescued, only more fatally, more horribly to lose her!

Thinking it probable that I was now on the eve of a full elucidation of circumstances, again my despondency was succeeded by the more violent passions; but I resolved to direct my eyes wholly towards the man, and narrowly to watch his motions. I saw him place the fowls in his basket, and pay the poulterer for them; he then walked away, and, at some distance, and much agitated, I followed him.

On quitting Rome I had, for the forwarding of my project, made some alterations in my usual manner of dressing; and afterwards, when I left Venice, my habit underwent a greater change: and I did not doubt but that it disguised my person, without attaching to it any singularity or appearance of affectation.

I drew my hat over my eyes, and pursued the object of my suspicion and curiosity, not only through the city, but also three or four miles beyond it. I was cautious in not seeming to notice him, and assumed an air of inattention to things which were around me, by carrying a book in my hand, and frequently looking at it. At length he turned out of the road, and entered a narrow and pleasant lane; I did the same with apparent indifference, and watched him into a small house or cottage that stood in a little adjacent meadow. I was at first prompted to rush forward, and break open the door which he had closed; but caution whispered that such an attempt would be absurd: and in order that I might not excite suspicion, I walked further down the lane, and at some considerable distance saw another small, but somewhat meaner house, where I thought I might venture a few enquiries.

I therefore walked up to it, at the same time hiding my emotions as much as possible, though I felt the flush of passion on my cheek, and knew that I had no direct power of changing or discolouring the growing hues. I took my hat from my head, as if

I were seeking refreshment from the air, and proceeded with an appearance of extreme fatigue and lassitude.

A young woman was sitting on a stool at the door, and I asked her for something cooling to refresh me;—she brought me fruit and ice; and after I had taken some of them, and made her a recompence, I started a few simple questions respecting the country, and afterwards others which related, though not particularly, to the inhabitants of the cottage that I had first noticed.

To the first enquiries she used a great deal of circumlocution, which I could well have dispensed with; and to the last; she could say but little. That little, however, roused me, and I drew still nearer to her, in order that my ear might take in every word as it passed from her.

"In that cottage, Signor," she replied, "lives a gentleman, who came to it scarcely more than a week ago."

"Indeed! so lately?"

"A day or two under or over, Signor. To those who love quiet it must be a pleasant place; I hope the stranger will find it such— with all my heart I wish it!"

"What is his name?" I enquired.

"I never heard it: I told you, Signor, that he was a stranger to me."

"Excuse me; I forgot it. Does he live alone? Has he any society?"

"He keeps a servant."

"Can you describe his person?"

"Of the servant, Signor?"

"No, of the master. I have a small curiosity; I think it is probable I shall know him."

"Why, as to describing him—I have seen him only twice, and even at those times not very perfectly; but I think he is a handsome, terrifying man. If ever a woman should love him, I am sure, very sure that she must likewise fear him."

"It is Salvini," I said incautiously, but somewhat indistinctly.

"What did you say?" enquired the girl.

"Nothing—only that your description is whimsical, and makes me laugh."

"I protest here comes the stranger now," said the cottager, rising from her stool.

"Where? where?" I exclaimed, while scorpions seemed to spring from my heart.

"Nay, now it is my turn to laugh at you, Signor. There, he is now coming from behind the large tree yonder; when he approaches, pray look at his dark visage and sullen brows."

"Not I," I replied; "I want not to see him."

"Whither is your curiosity gone, Signor?" said the girl, with more mirth than suspicion.

"I had none," I answered; "I was only sporting with you. With your leave I will step into your cottage, and rest myself awhile."

"Do so," she said; "I must, however, have another peep at the stranger; when he is gone by, I will come and dispose my mother's couch for you."

I stepped hastily into the cottage, and putting aside a small part of the window curtain, panting and agitated, watched for the stranger. I saw him at the distance of several yards, and instantly knew him to be Salvini. I looked at the villain's face: it was dark and contracted; and though his eyes fell on the cottager, who was young and blooming, their fires were not softened.

My veins in a moment were swelling, and in the succeeding one my blood was curdled. I was starting forward to pursue and stab him; but my sinews relaxed, my legs failed me, and my head fell with violence upon a table that stood by my side.

The cottager at that instant entered, and looking earnestly at me, enquired whether I was not well; to which I answered that I believed I had been somewhat incautious in eating so much of her fruit and ice when the temperature of my body was so hot and moist. In order to prevent any ill effects arising, my kind young hostess offered me a cordial, and pressed it upon me with so much kindness and force of recommendation, that I could not decline it.

In a few minutes after I declared myself much recovered, at the same time attributing, as she did, the favourable change to the virtues of the draught she had given me. I did not offer her any reward, but slipped a small purse, without her perceiving it, into the glass which I had used; when putting it aside, I bade my lively little friend adieu, and departed from the cottage.

The free air somewhat revived me; and having walked a little distance, I stopped, in order to think of my plans and means of operation.

What should I do respecting Salvini? Give him up to the law? Was it certain that he would suffer by it? Neither fine nor imprisonment were in a thousandth degree adequate to his villany.— Meet him arm to arm, breast to breast? What, place myself in equal terms before the ravisher of my wife? before her murderer? perhaps to fall the victim of chance, and consequently add to his former brutal triumph? No, no! Should I shoot him, stab him? Yes, yes! To remove such a monster would not be a mere gratification of my revenge and awakened passions; but it would also be to benefit society, and take off a most vile and corruptive blot from human nature, which would look the fairer for the action.

I determined, vowed, most solemnly swore that, within the space of a few hours, he should die by my hand—by the hand of the husband of Rosolie.—Angel! I thought I heard your soft voice in the clouds approving my oath; I even looked up for you towards Heaven, but my eyes, having strained themselves in disappointment, only fell on the paths which had been so lately trodden by your destroyer. "Retribution is near, spirit!" I cried—"retribution is at hand! You will hear of it above; it will be rumoured by the shuddering Saints, and I shall soon be with you to announce it!"

I returned to Milan, and purchased at one shop a brace of pistols, some powder, and balls; and at another place I provided myself with a stiletto, as I had not fully determined which of the two instruments I should use in the dispatching of my enemy. I wished not to be ingeniously sanguinary, though I could not abate him an atom of my vengeance. Putting my new purchases into my pocket, I again left the city, and journeying back to the village, loitered about till some considerable time after sunset.

I afterwards approached the cottage of Salvini; but seeing the servant employed in the little garden, I again retired some distance from the premises, without attracting his notice, or drawing his attention from his work. It was my design to make a deliberate sacrifice, and therefore I wished not to enter into any engagement or contest; on that night I firmly resolved to cleanse Salvini's body of his foul spirit however hazardous the attempt might be, and whoever witnessed my actions, or had the temerity to oppose them. Fidelity, perhaps, might bind the servant to the master; but that I considered as no obstacle, even should they not be apart from each other when I rushed forward to seize my prey. The powers of resolution were great within me; the strength of many men seemed at that hour to be at my command; and I had not a doubt but that one of my arms would be able to shoot or to stab Salvini, while the other grasped his menial, and kept him at its full length from me. Had it been possible for them both to have assumed the forms of lions, I should not have feared, in that hour of inspiration, their shaggy paws, or been put to flight by their united roarings.

My mind was firm; I felt not the compunctions of horror; I did not view myself as a designing murderer, neither did I tremble when I cast up my eyes to the realms of the Supreme Spirit, whose ken is said to be illimitable. Never had a malefactor, doomed by the violated laws of his country to expire in public beneath the instruments of torture, committed crimes more atrocious—crimes, which the ear of humanity would turn from, and the soul sicken at!

I again went towards the cottage, and when I was within a few yards of it, saw Salvini and his servant standing at the door: they had been, and were still conversing together.

"That you can do," said the former, alluding to something which had preceded—"that you can do in the morning when you go to Milan; and I would not have you forget to bring with you the opiates; tell the apothecary to make them more powerful, for his others were weak, and had no effect."

"Ah, ha!" I cried, or rather strongly thought, "is it so? I have the means to quiet you and your compunctions, and will apply them too."

"And tell him," Salvini continued, "that, during the night, a fever preys strongly on me, and that I wish him to send——no, tell him to come to me in the course of a day or two. You may desire that he will return with you on the morrow."

"Yes, Signor, I shall be back at noon."

"That is sufficient; open the window of my chamber; I shall walk awhile, and return about eleven."

"What will you take for supper, Signor?" enquired the man.

"Any thing—nothing—I shall not eat to-night."

"Nor to-morrow night, nor at any time hereafter," said I, mentally.

Salvini walked into the garden; I heard him sigh, as if he were much oppressed. He entered a little arbour, but staid in it scarcely a minute; he then plucked a rose from a tree that grew very near the hedge behind which I had concealed myself; he smelt of the flower, gazed on it earnestly, and sighing still more heavily, threw it from him.

He surely at that moment thought of Rosolie, of the blossom that opened and flourished under his eye, the sweet rose which he should have tenderly nourished and fostered, but which he rifled, withered, blasted!

"And blasted be thee, thou false friend, thou cruel guardian, thou most abandoned villain!"

I did not then shoot him; but seeing him pass the gate, I moved from my hiding-place, and followed him at a distance. I felt for my stiletto, which was in my bosom, and placed it in such a manner that an instant might not be lost in drawing it from the scabbard; my pistols were in my pocket, their barrels well filled with powder and balls; every thing was ready for my purpose.

Night never was more beautiful; the scattered lamps of Heaven burnt clear; the hills, the meadows, and the trees were silvered; and the shadow of Salvini fell a great length on the ground, and served me as a guide.——

"Look around, wretch, and the beauties of nature, perhaps, may give you a momentary pleasure; look up, murderer, and wonder at the magnificence of God! of him, into whose regions you shall never enter; of him, whose eye shall be as lightning to you! Confess yourself, tremble, sue for mercy, that, if forbidden to claim one of the joys of Heaven, you may not be driven into the caverns of hell! Pray, if it avail you nothing, pray! You see the moon shedding a world of light; you shall not see it to-morrow rise over the hills! You hear the bird of night pouring forth its melody, and sending its clear notes through the vales of innocence; some few strains more, and then your ears shall shut out all sound for ever! The spirits of the elements are blowing sweetly in your face; but within an hour they shall pass over your breathless and unconscious body! The gulph of oblivion is yawning, and the sinews of my arm are swelling to hurl you into it!"

He still continued to walk, and I to follow. He had gone nearly a mile from his house, when he entered a small grove, or clump of trees. The moment was come! I hastened my steps, placed myself before him, and bound my fingers like curves of iron round his arm.

He hastily enquired who I was.

"Roncorone!" I replied—"Roncorone!"

"Oh Heaven!" he exclaimed, and endeavoured, but in vain, to free himself from my violent grasp.

"Salvini," I said, "use no efforts to release yourself; did you possess treble strength, my arms should still hold you. Struggle not; I came hither not to be baffled, but to——"

"To do what?" said the guilty wretch, faltering and trembling almost to annihilation.

"To give you a passport to the world which is at present unknown to you; to make a speedy division between your soul and body."

"To kill me! to murder me!"

"To sacrifice you! Such is my intention—such the purpose that brought me hither."

He again attempted to release himself, but I drew forth one of my pistols and placing it near his head, he struggled no more. He however became despicably abject; and, throwing himself on his knees, begged for mercy.

"What!" I exclaimed, "mercy from *me*? mercy from the husband of Rosolie? Villain! that name has roused me. Detested fiend! can you expect mercy from me? Dare you look for it from God? But here, before this instrument levels you, confess yourself; if words will procure you pardon, speak them; however, be brief, for all your faculties will end in the space of ten minutes. Confess——"

"What, what should I confess?"

"That your heart has long been the receptacle of vice; that your past deeds have been horrible enough to doom you to hell; that you are a murderer—a ravisher! Confess, confess!"

"I will not; who can thus arraign me?"

"Were my father living, he could do it; and would not the

deceased and mistaken Venzone join his evidence? Stephano, that dark and cruel devil, resembling yourself, could speak to it—Lucilla—my wife, my wife, fiend! all could accuse you. Have I struck you dumb? Speak instantly, or my fury may even spurn at a momentary restraint!"

"Hear me," he cried—"hear me, Roncorone! My actions indeed have not been just, but they have been greatly exaggerated. Stephano was a rascal, Lucilla a bawd, and their evidence therefore ought not to convict me. Your wife, had she lived, I should have restored to you."

"Filthy villain! what, stained, deflowered?"

"By whom? Not by me. Roncorone, your ear has been grossly abused by lies."

"And is at this moment. Confess—you set my house on fire?"

"I did. Pardon, pardon me for it!"

"You imposed on my wife with falsehood, seized her, carried her to Rome."

"It is true. I beseech you forgive me!"

"And there you ravished her!"

"Oh, no, no!"

"You did, monster! You forced her, compelled her; you placed a soil on her innocence, marked her with pollution, brought death upon her!"

"No, indeed, indeed——"

"Liar! hell demands you of me!"

I threw him on his back and having grappled with him for a moment, discharged the contents of one of my pistols into his head. It was not wholly effectual, for he afterwards murmured— "I am guilty! I am guilty!" when I placed the barrel of the other instrument to his mouth, and scattered his brains.

I threw the pistols from me, and they fell into a pool of water near the spot which was marked with the blood of Salvini; my stiletto followed them, for I had no more death-deeds to perform. My work accomplished, and my designs effected, I removed the stains from my hands, and leaving the grove, took the road leading to Milan. I however loitered about the suburbs of the city, and did not enter it till the morning, when I returned to my lodging, apparently tranquil, though internally agitated.

* * * * * *

I sat down, alone and undisturbed, to think on what had passed. I did not shrink from my actions; I would not, had I possessed the power, have given Salvini his life again; and when I reflected on his death, I murmured, "Such be the end of every atrocious villain like himself!"

Oh, what ideas followed next! But for him, happiness and bliss had still been mine! but for him, I had been an husband, ever receiving from my soft partner love, tenderness, ecstacy! nay, perhaps, but for his—Oh God!—but for his violation, I had been a father, listening to the plaints of my babe, or fondly gazing on its little face of smiling innocence! Ah! wretched and most miserable Roncorone!

* * * * * *

I left Milan on the following day, and before any rumours had gone forth respecting the transaction in which I had been concerned. My intention was, as it had been before the discovery of my wife at Rome, and when I was bewailing her supposed death, to seclude myself from the world, to seek some spot where the inhabitants were few, and where the malice, cunning, and duplicity of the thicker swarm were not to be traced. I wished to find a place of quiet, where my tired spirit might sink into its long sleep, untainted by loquacity, and unmolested by these effusions which cost worldly sensibility only a short breathing, common as the air, but dispensing none of its benefits.

In past visionary moments I had regarded the world as a noble temple, canopied with beautiful architecture, and tenanted by minor Gods! Wherever I then turned, I beheld, or fancied I beheld, Virtue and Charity employed in their deeds of goodness, Mercy stretching forth her hands, and Truth smiling brighter than the sun, which she could look at unblinking; Science receiving reward, Genius unexacted admiration, and Philanthropy—benign Philanthropy! giving smiles to the faces of thousands, pleasure to the hearts of millions! Oh, how beautiful was every thing to the eye! how heavenly every thing to the imagination!

But the optics are only the intelligencers to the soul, to that emporium in which the ingredients of our passions, of our affections, and of our antipathies are indiscriminately placed, in order to be modelled by worldly occurrences. The world—that world which once had so charmed and ravished me, now appeared no more than a mortifying spectacle, darkened in some parts by the general frailties of man, in others ensanguined by his crimes, but in none irradiated by his virtues. My former opinions being again considered, were found to arise from infatuation; but I confess when I discovered how far I had gone astray, I sighed at the necessity of retracting. There is something even to regret and mourn for when we are recalled from pleasing deceptions by painful and melancholy truths; we wish almost to be lulled into them again, when the powers that roused us offer no real for the artificial good. Cold Philosophy will spurn at this, because she teaches that truth is always good, always excellent.

My affairs were few, and easily to be arranged; I posted back to Venice, where, in privacy, I settled them all preparatory to my renunciation of society. I discovered myself only to my agent, who was rewarded for his secrecy; he collected my property, and having reserved a sufficient sum for the poor necessities of my few coming days, or years, as it might be, I assigned the remainder by a writing to my friend Alberti, and charged him only with the guardianship of a young orphan, a little boy, whom I had snatched from the storms of adversity, and the fangs of poverty, and whose innocent tongue used, every time I saw him, to say, "Heaven bless Signor Roncorone!"—"Endeavour to make your charge an honest and worthy man," I said in the paper which I addressed to Alberti; "I hope he will be rising to manhood with promise, and you declining into age with tranquillity, when the planks of my coffin, if any man shall provide me with one, will be rotten, and disjoined by the creatures of the earth. The boy has too many sensibilities—blunt the edges of some of them; stupidity ensures happiness better than excess of feeling."

I appropriated a sum of money for a monument to be erected

to the memory of my wife; and in a letter entreated Alberti to attend personally to the performance of this business.

Oh spirit of peace! no epitaph could do thee justice! the sons of Art could never raise a monument so durable as that which was contained in the soul of thy distracted husband. The one must necessarily yield to time and to the sway of years; but the other not prolonged centuries, nor elemental blasts, nor the last great convulsions of nature could throw down, or in any manner efface. God! at that moment I felt thy magnitude; and the expansion of thy power enraptured me while I, trembling, gazed upon thy bright dominions!

It was a pain to part from my little *protegé*; he asked me why I sighed, why my cheeks were so pale, why I had not seen him for so long a time, and where the dear Signora, meaning my wife, then was; and when I kissed him, and told him I was going, he clasped my neck, and sobbed out, "God bless you, Signor! when will you again come back to Ferdinand?"—The boy's words found the chords of my sensibility, and played exquisitely upon them. I fondled him till he fell asleep in my arms, when I laid him gently on a couch, and kissing his red lips, gave him a last look, and left him for ever.

After a private residence in Venice of a fortnight, I departed from thence, in order to carry my debilitated body and ruined mind to Switzerland; in which country I meant to dwell as long as local habitation was of any consideration to me. Having formed the design of making a voyage, I embarked at Venice, and afterwards entered the mouth of the Po, it being my intention to go up that river as far as Cremona, for the fatigue of travelling was at that time too great for me.

The beauties of Nature no longer could fascinate or even please my eye; it was dead to them, though the time had been when it would have stretched with enthusiasm. I was not charmed by the undulation of the waves, or by the rich and varied prospects on the banks of the river; nor could the evening chantings of the mariners, nor the more lively strains of the peasants, which came from the opposite shores, give me the most transitory sensation of pleasure, or purge my imagination of the foulness that hung over it like a fog. My powers were decaying; the faculties, which solely constitute the riches of life, and without which not even the airs of Heaven seem worth inhaling, were falling languidly and separating in sickness, and I made no effort either to recal or recollect them.

I did not disembark at Cremona, as I had intended, but sailed to Pavia, where I landed, and from whence I designed to depart on the following day.

The next morning, however, I found myself unable to proceed; my indisposition increased most rapidly, and my giddiness was so great, that even motionless things seemed to move fantastically before my eyes. I thought I was dying; and in that thought there was pleasure, otherwise a considerable degree of satisfaction.— "The moment is nearly come!" I cried; "I am about to associate with angels—to open my eyes on all the grandeur and mysteries of the universal God!"—I smiled in my sickness, and was as unruffled by fear as I had ever been in the calmest hour of infancy.

I was, however, deceived in my expectations; for the time of perpetual silence was not yet at hand. I had not been in Pavia more than six or seven days when the vertigo ceased, and health again strove to effect an establishment.

But my plagues and miseries ended not here; Fate was planning most craftily for me, and preparing a damnable web to catch me in.

I had not been out of my inn since my debarkation, but my host and his family had been very attentive and tender to me, and they expressed much pleasure on my recovery; I felt the kindness of these people—very sensibly felt it, though I could have wished never to hear such congratulations. They were one day speaking of an execution that was to take place at Milan on the next day; and being present, and seeing that the subject created much interest among them, I enquired the nature of the offence, and was told it was that of murder.

"The name of the culprit," continued my landlord, "is Luzzi; he was in the service of Signor Salvini, whom he murdered some little time ago; for which crime, and an horrid one it was, he is to-morrow to die on the wheel."

"God!"

"Signor?"

"What proofs were there of his guilt?"

"Oh, most convincing proofs! evident, palpable! such as the shallow cunning of the wretch could not shift from the eyes of the world and justice."

"Indeed, indeed! Pray what were they?"

"Why Signor Salvini lived in retirement; he had been but a short time in that part of the country; he was found murdered at some little distance from his dwelling, and many articles of considerable value were afterwards discovered in the boxes of the villain, who had not fled before the alarm was given, and who, on being apprehended, freely acknowledged the theft, but most obstinately denied the murder."

"Oh! and is there no other evidence against him?"

"No other, Signor;—surely this is sufficient."

"And he is to die?"

"The rack ends him to-morrow."

In one moment I felt the pangs of a thousand dying men, and, sinking into a chair, sat some considerable time in a stupor; at length, recollecting myself, I ordered that post-horses might be immediately prepared to take me to Milan.

My agitation, I perceived, astonished my host, who was desirous of asking me some questions concerning the cause of it; but I silenced him, and afterwards sent him to look after the conveyance that I had ordered, and into which, in the course of half an hour, I threw myself, in order to be driven from Pavia. My drivers assured me that I should be in Milan soon after sunset; but owing to an injury done to the vehicle, and to the wretched state of the horses, it was near ten o'clock when I reached that city, and I could therefore enter into no part of my business till the morning.

My first enquiry was at what time the execution would take place on the morrow; and being informed that the criminal would be brought forth at the hour of ten, I retired to my chamber, though my limbs almost refused to perform their accustomed offices.

I dismissed the person who attended me to my sleeping room, without ordering, or even thinking of any refreshment for myself. I placed the lamp on a table, and threw my hands upon my heated forehead. A large mirror was in the front of me; my eyes glanced upon it, but I withdrew them in terror, as the glass seemed to cast upon me the pale manacled victim, the grim, unpitying execution-ers, and all the dreadful apparatus of the limb-tearing wheel. I altered my position, but even then I could not banish the appalling figures of imagination.

My thoughts were growing wild. The danger of the pris-oner,—the horror of such a punishment falling on the innocent,— the knowledge of a man's mind, when his situation is desperate, suggesting desperate means of extricating himself,—suicide how often preferred, if the necessary aids are within reach, to a public, prolonged, and excruciating death! These were the subjects, the dreadful subjects which were incessantly shifting in my mind.

The time till the morning seemed almost half a century, and I thought light more tardy than usual. In the interim, however, I had formed my principal design, which was to rescue the condemned man by a confession of my own guilt, which could alone preserve him, and also to throw myself upon the laws, the severity of which I did not fear, and the mercy of which I resolved not to court.

To preserve so wretched a life as mine, so burthened an exis-tence,—to keep in action senses which stirred not at the call of happiness, and still were never resting, should I, *could* I suffer inno-cence to writhe under the torture, after hearing the curses of the unfeeling multitude assembled to gape upon the agonies of one of the Almighty's creatures?

He might have a wife; should I send her into the world dis-tracted? He might be a father; God of the universe! should I cause the throats of his babes to scream, their innocent bosoms to heave convulsively, their poor, poor eyes to overflow, and their guileless tongues to say to each other—"Our father is butchered! his veins are emptied, his limbs bruised, broken, and disjointed! let us weep, sisters,—let us mourn, brothers, for our parent is cruelly torn from us for ever!"

Had I for a moment harboured such a design, I should have wished that never thereafter the ears of Heaven would be, *even for a moment*, inclined to my supplications.

I was in the streets soon after the hour of seven; there were then nearly three hours to pass before that which had been appointed for the execution, and consequently sufficient time for me to go before an officer of justice, or a magistrate, and to make a confession of those actions which it was now horrid, inhuman, and even devilish to conceal.

I stopped not to ponder on my designs, but hurried through the streets till I arrived at the house of a magistrate, to whom I had been directed. He was not risen. Anxious to see and speak to him, I entreated a servant (making my request more forcible by the application of a piece of money) to go up to his chamber, and inform him that a person was waiting to make a very important discovery, which, if not immediately attended to, would be productive of the most dreadful consequences that could possibly be conceived.

I believe the man suspected that my intellects were impaired. After looking at me a short time, and putting my present into his pocket, he however went up with my message, and in about ten minutes returned and acquainted me that his master would attend me as soon as he could put on his clothes.

I was well satisfied with the answer, I endeavoured to collect myself against the appearance of the magistrate, and to make my self-accusations with firmness: but my mind recurred to the shocking situation of the condemned prisoner, and my agitation again became violent.

The person for whom I was waiting, now entered the room, and viewing me very attentively, enquired my early business.

"I have a serious charge to make," I replied—"a very serious, and I doubt not but that you will say a very dreadful charge."

"Against whom?"

"Myself—my accusation goes no further; I am come to state my own deeds to you."

"Then I dare believe your criminality is not great."

"Dare *not* believe it; you are deceived; it is perhaps of such a nature as will shew me of a devil's colour to your eyes."

"Extraordinary! proceed, Signor."

"There is a man doomed to the wheel this morning."

"I know it."

"Doomed for murder."

"True; he is to give his own blood for that which he spilt."

"Touch not a limb of him—not a single limb! let not the hand of the executioner even go near to him. The crime of which he is accused, for which he is condemned to suffer, he is as innocent of as the purest of the saints were of the crucifixion of Christ! Hear me, attend to me—*he is* not, but *I am* the murderer."

"The murderer of Salvini?"

"Yes, of Salvini. These hands, spotless as they now appear, brought death on him, gave him his last passport, and sent him to hell, his fittest residence. But pardon me—I talk rudely."

"Do you talk *truly*, Signor?"

"Do you believe in God? in the Son of the Holy Virgin?"

"Most firmly!" replied the magistrate, raising his cross—"most devoutly!"

"So do I; and as truly as I believe in them, so truly am I the murderer of Salvini. Hasten to the prison, release the culprit, and place me in his dungeon. I heard not of his situation till yesterday; had I been acquainted with his captivity as soon as it commenced, I swear he should not have pined a single day. Be quick, be quick, or it may be too late!"

"It is, I fear, *now* too late; the confession should, I apprehend, have been made before, if it were really designed to avert the punishment of the supposed criminal."

"Why—why? The hour fixed for his death is that of ten, is it not?"

"It was afterwards altered. He suffers at eight; your self-accusation therefore is undoubtedly too late to save the prisoner."

My blood becoming instantly cold, I shivered as if the different members of my body were parting.

"Murder!" I exclaimed; "follow me to the scaffold! follow me instantly! I shall be damned indeed if Luzzi has suffered! I would not bring death on him to be sovereign of the world!"

I ran out of the house, and though little acquainted with the city, had to make no enquiries respecting the place of death, as I saw many people hastening towards it. I was the swiftest of the swift, and it was not long before I arrived at the murderous spot.

The crowd was immense, the dreadful apparatus prepared, the convict partly bound on the wheel, and a tormenting priest stood preaching in the language of damnation, in order to extort a confession of crimes of which the poor wretch was not guilty. I could not get near to the scaffold, but I called out loudly and repeatedly,

"Kill not the innocent! kill not the innocent!" when my words or my gestures raised the mirth of the hardened bye-standers; many of whom indulged themselves with bursts of laughter, and with expressions so gross, shocking, and inapplicable, that they irritated and disgusted me.

I removed to some little distance, repeating with more force and exertion the same words; but they had not any greater effect. At that moment I heard a dreadful shriek from the victim, a thousand sobs and murmurs from the spectators. This was too mighty a blow for me; I was growing mad.

"Stop the execution!" I vociferated; "I have a pardon!"

"Pardon! pardon! pardon!" resounded through the crowd. I took advantage of their credulity, and holding up a folded paper, the people joyfully gave way, and made a passage for me to the scaffold. I eagerly mounted the ladder that was placed against it, and threw myself on the wheel; but hearing a deeper groan than any that had before reached me, and seeing blood running on the planks, my eyes shut themselves up in horror and grief, and my senses were instantly and entirely suspended. Before they again became active, I was removed from the scaffold, and afterwards I found myself in a room surrounded by several persons. The magistrate to whom I had applied, and who had followed me from his house with all possible speed, as I had directed, was among them, and to him I first addressed myself.

My earliest question was concerning the tortured, and my eyes filled with the tears of pleasure and of humanity when I was informed that the sentence, owing to my very strange and unprecedented confession, had no further fallen on him than by breaking one of his arms. That, indeed, was a shocking injury, but I was glad not to hear it aggravated.

On being asked whether I still persisted in my recent acknowledgment, I desired a solemn oath to be administered to me; which being done, I again said that I was the murderer of Salvini, and the only person employed in the transaction. I described the spot, the hour, and, recollecting myself, spoke of the water in which I had thrown the pistols and stiletto. If this evidence were not sufficient, I referred them to my host at Milan, who could speak of my absence on that particular night, and also to the cottager, who had seen me near the place of action some few hours before I had shot Salvini.

On being asked the cause of my deeds, for a short time I remained silent; at length, however, I told my examiner that my motives should not be revealed, and that the law should proceed in its regular course on the full and, as I supposed, sufficient confession of my guilt. The people around me looked much surprised, and wondered at my extraordinary conduct; but neither entreaties nor threats could wring the secret from me, or make me speak of the wrongs of my wife. I found it impossible to touch on a theme like that; my soul revolted at it. I was consequently sent to the prison, and lodged in a dungeon, in order to take my trial for the murder of Salvini.

The legal thieves robbed me of all my money; they however allowed me to retain a few papers, which were to them unimportant, and, in spite of their sagacity, I concealed from them a miniature of Rosolie. It was very richly set with diamonds; but to me the most valuable part was the painting, so truly like, so justly resembling my dear, my beloved wife! My heart beat with pleasure when the keeper left my cell without discovering my treasure, which I immediately hid within an aperture of one of the walls in the darkest corner of the prison room.—Trifles sometimes will alleviate the pangs of the wretched, particularly if sensibility has a distinguished claim upon their hearts; and *my heart* was cheered, was solaced by the idea of carrying the picture of my murdered wife in my fond bosom to the scaffold, where the rack would probably crush it with my existence; but I frequently went to the place of its concealment, took it from thence, placed it for a moment in the strongest light which the narrow grate afforded, and casting my eyes upon it for an instant, deposited it again, lest I might be surprised, and lose it. Oh memory! thou hast more pains than pleasures, more curses than delights!

* * * * * *

The man whom I had snatched from the wheel, was likely soon to recover; and though he had acknowledged himself a thief, his punishment was deemed sufficient, and he was therefore discharged. Previous to his leaving the prison, he was admitted into my cell; he instantly knew me, but did not vent a single reproach. I expressed the sorrow that I really felt for having been the cause of his disgrace and sufferings, entreated him to forgive me for it, and assured him that, previous to my death, I would give directions for every possible reparation to be made to him by one of my surviving friends.

I wished for a speedy trial, and was gratified; for after passing a fortnight in my dungeon, I was brought before my judges. As I had directed, the three witnesses whom I had named, were in the court. One of them stated my purchase of the pistols and stiletto; another proved my absence from his house during all the night in which the murder was committed; and the last, the female cottager, who now looked on me most expressively, spoke of my being in the village, and repeated the conversation I had held with her in the early part of the day.

Having persisted in concealing my motives for killing Salvini, and solemnly repeated my former confession of my guilt, a sentence similar to that of the former unfortunate culprit was passed upon me.

I rose, and bowed to the man who had pronounced it.

"I hear your decree with calmness," I cried; "I shudder not at it, for death brings to me no terrors, no apprehensions. I have performed my duty in acknowledging the deed; you have done the same in condemning me for the perpetration of it. I know the eyes of every person around me view me as a monster; I know that those who shall witness my dissolution, will direct to me their scorn, and load me with opprobrium. Let them; still will I indulge the privilege of secrecy;—not one of those curious machines, which are made to give an exquisite sense to torture, shall make me cry out—'Spare me, and I will confess.' Regard me not for this declaration as a hardened villain; indeed I am not such, nor have I ever deserved so harsh an appellation; but if my heart were to feel the least repugnance for what my hands have done, those very hands should afterwards be employed in tearing it from my breast. Oh! I *could* tell a tale, that fathers, husbands, mothers, wives, nay, even children would weep at, which would dissolve the most inflexible heart, and make my censurers pitiers. Oh, so horrid! but my firmness is affected. If there be a hell, Salvini's soul is in the midst of it; and as there is a heaven, I fear not but that I, ere long, shall discover it. Lead me to my dungeon!"

I saw tears, and heard sobbings, and my judges looked mildly on me as I left the court.

Having regained my cell, I became more composed; and by the time that my chain was adjusted, and my door secured, my heart was considerably less agitated.

I had seven days to live; had they been only hours, I should have been happier. Considering my situation, I was not treated inhumanly, nor loaded with superfluous fetters; my gaoler, indeed, used precaution in securing me, but he did not want to weigh my body down with irons. I regarded him with no malignity or severity for what he did; on the contrary, I spoke mildly, and sometimes gratefully to him. I did not obstinately reject the food he brought to me, though I was scarcely sensible of the quality or flavour of it; and, at my earnest intercession, he supplied me with materials for writing.

After some reflections, and they indeed were serious ones, I began to write an account of what I had hitherto concealed, which I knew would be soon fully corroborated by my friend Alberti. Had I wished for life, there was a great probability of obtaining a pardon, as the evidence of Alberti and Lucilla would have confirmed my statement of circumstances, and, in a great degree, tended to remove my criminality; but breathing being oppressive to me, and my soul longing for a state of eternal quiet, I only hoped that my situation would remain unknown to my best worldly friend until my fate was decided on the scaffold. Any interposition on his part would have afflicted me greatly, and his presence would certainly have overpowered me and all my fortitude.

Two days passed away, and no person appeared before me, except the gaoler and the Confessor who attended the condemned of the prison. The kindness of the former I returned with gratitude, as it was truly exemplary; but the latter I dismissed, having first assured him, though not with the tone of rudeness, that I never had entertained a favourable opinion of receiving any benefit in telling to a Priest what I feared, or was disinclined to avow to all my fellows of the earth. This put him to flight; and it was evident that the churl considered me as doomed to perdition, not merely for the crime for which I was manacled, but also for my heresy and disbelief of the powers and virtues of his function.— "Go thy ways, gloomy and dark-browed Monk!" I said, as he went in anger from my cell; "I shall not trust my cause with thee; while I can appeal to God myself, I will employ no other person to do it in my behalf."

I still continued to write, and the time to pass; four of the seven days had gone over, and preparations were making for the closing one. My narrative, painful as the task was, was carried on regularly till I came to account for the murder of Salvini. There I paused, and fell into a train of reflections which surprised even myself; for they were subversive of all the principles that I had been endeavouring to establish, and of the fortitude that I had been implanting.

I entered into self-argument. Dying on the wheel had now some weight with me, and I began to lothe the idea of going out of the world amidst curses and execrations; and there appeared something truly horrid in having my lacerated body held forth in a disgusting manner to public view.

These ideas oppressed me, and I found that I had been a boaster and an hypocrite; for, though I feared not death, I shrank from the idea of my marrow being pressed out of my splintered bones. I laid down my pen, and sighed to think that I could not have the privilege of rotting in the earth. Afterwards, however, I endeavoured to banish these weak thoughts; but it was impossible; my stability was shaken, and my fortitude not to be again raised.

Night came on, and I was involved in darkness, the use of a lamp being denied me; the prison was growing silent, and I heard only a faint noise, which I supposed to be occasioned by the rats in the earth. I hoped to recover my strength of resolution before the morning, but could make no immediate progress in it; my food and hard bed were neglected, and I sat on my stone seat till the clock struck twelve.

I was growing faint with my ideas. "Must I, indeed," I exclaimed aloud, "die with torture and ignominy for the extirpation of such a villain?"

"Can you be brave?" said a voice; "if so, live and be at liberty."

Starting, I enquired who it was that thus strangely addressed me.

"A friend who will serve you," was the answer.

"Where? In my dungeon?"

"No, a mole beneath it. Be honest, be firm! Halloo! your help here. Hush! the watch! the watch!"

I heard a noise under the floor, but silence succeeded, and I remained in amazement for the space of half an hour, when the invisible again addressed me, and immediately after I saw a faint gleam of light, and also one of the broad stones, with which my dungeon was paved, lifted up by degrees, and at length carefully removed.

A tall man raised himself from the hole, and allowing his lanthorn to give a greater light, he approached me, and smiling, tendered me his hand. Amazement still possessed me, and my eyes were fixed on the face of the stranger, who was a young man, possessing much grace and beauty.

"You are sentenced to die, Signor?" he said.

"I am within a few days to die," I replied.

"And it is repugnant to you?" he said, smiling. "Well, I allow it is not unnatural."

"To die by the hands of a common executioner is indeed repugnant to me."

"Damned be he who attempts to crush you," he exclaimed; "but this place suits not vehemence. I think, Signor, for I have heard something of your character—I think to the man who is, and wishes to prove himself your friend, that you could be——"

"A friend. I could—I swear it!"

"It is enough. Sincerity (I am no fool of compliments) has finely drawn her lines upon your countenance; I will confide in you, and account for my strange appearance. I have been confined in an adjoining cell upwards of seven months; and it was on the condition of breathing the purity of its air for the term of seven years, which you will allow is a considerable gap in a man's life, that the dogs of Milan restrained their agents from pulling me piecemeal for the amusement of a fight-loving populace.

"I was accused of having spoken certain words against the Senate, or the Viceroy, or the house of—— But a truce with accusations: Patriots have in all ages bled; even traitors have been known to demand—aye, and to *receive* the badge of honour. A niggardly villain, a thief of confidence, put me into the hands of justice, as it is called, and being declared guilty of the imputed charges, sentence was immediately passed on me; and though it was afterwards mitigated, I had, in a filthy prison, to bear the heats of seven summers, the colds of as many winters, to feast on the blood-correcting aliments, and either to walk or to dance, as my fancy might direct me, within the circle allowed by, and to the music of, my own chains.

"Signor! my buoyant spirits were not to be depressed. In my captivity my heart beat nobly, and I was as great as any of the ephemera, whom I was accused of having slandered; and my mind was not imprisoned, for it wandered from system to system, and dwelt on present and on future prospects. But hark! hush! Did you not hear a noise? No, all is silent.

"My private history," he continued, "would not much interest you."

"You are deceived," I replied; "I should attend to the relation of it with great earnestness."

"Aye, but the time is unapt. I shall therefore only say that my father was a very eminent chemist:—he had imparted some of his knowledge to me; and being allowed to retain a few of his books and manuscripts in prison, the gaining of further information in the art was my principal solace; and perhaps, at this moment, I am the possessor of such mysteries as the students and practitioners of all Italy are unacquainted with. But more of this in another place.

"I was soon disgusted with my confinement; but the prevention of liberty could not, as I said before, affect the vigour of my mind: and though thick walls inclosed, and irons bound me, I meditated an escape. For the first three months no person, except the gaoler, was allowed to enter my dungeon; but as I behaved with what the men of power called propriety, I was afterwards allowed to throw my arms, and with them my chains, around the necks of such friends as had not forgotten me. You will probably smile when I tell you that my most constant visiter was a woman; not my daughter—I am too young; not my wife—I never was married.

It was a woman who lived with and loved me; not by the rules of duty and obedience, but by those of free passions and affections—a woman whose mind and body corresponded intimately with my own. Think me not an egot for the last words that I spoke, if I add to them, she was a noble creature, rivalled by none of ancient—equalled, I believe, by none of modern times—one who could *almost*, (I do not say *wholly*) Signor, with her own hands, lay her heart a sacrifice on the altar of friendship. Brave woman! excellent creature!

"Pardon me for these flights, and do not think me hyperbolical. She bore me two boys at a birth. Oh! could you but see the fire of their little eyes, and the early expression of their plastic features! In each of them I behold an epitome of greatness. May the winds of prosperity blow on them in their youth, and Glory become their patroness when they shall go into the world as men!—as men of strength, of zeal, and of enterprise; not as puppets in fantoccini, nor as Italian macaroni, grinning in pocket mirrors, and acquiring shrill voices at the expence of their manhood.

"Apollonia cursed the rigour of my judges as much as I did; she was not in the habit of weeping and swooning—a habit which many of her sex adopt in the very moments when resolution is most requisite, and which mere chagrin or petulance will often draw them into; but she felt not the less for my situation, and my chains wounded her as much as myself. By her ingenuity, however, I was enabled to lighten them; for unbraiding her fine hair one day, she took from under it a couple of small files, with which I made niches in my irons just large enough to pass the links. This was a step towards freedom;—I knew the hours of my gaoler's visits; whenever he came, therefore, he found me apparently confined, and placed in a corresponding attitude; but in his absence I was the free ranger of my realm. I was also as unbroken in my spirit as the rewarded patriot who brought me to my present state, and whose body, should I ever hereafter meet with him, I will, or may I become more despicable than a dog that grubs in alleys!——but whither am I going?—I will damn him, and then return!

"The same dear and friendly hand that had furnished me with the files, supplied me with several other small implements, and likewise pointed out a place to conceal them in; for she had as many projects as a minister, but they were of a more worthy nature.

"With some difficulty we raised a stone, and to our surprise found a hollow space beneath it; I did not then enter it, but put the covering carefully over it, as I intended to reserve my observations till some fitter season. Apollonia, however, as well as myself, was anxious to know how it terminated, and ardently wished that it might lead me to liberty.

"Having discovered this depository, Apollonia, on the following day, brought me some phosphorus, a small lanthorn, and matches, and the ensuing midnight I descended into the passage, which, to my mortification, I found only of the length of a few feet, and its depth was very inconsiderable. The bubbles of hope burst, and for a few moments I was extremely chagrined; the depression, however, was of no long date, and I laughed over the matter when I again saw my noble-minded associate. Liberty! I still panted for liberty! and in order to obtain it, I entered into an arduous and fatiguing undertaking, which was to divert the course of the passage, and to turn it towards the court that fronted the door of my cell. If I were to be discovered in this attempt, should I not be punished with the utmost severity, removed to a dungeon still more damp and ugly, drag many additional chains, and be deprived of the sight and converse of my faithful Apollonia? I desisted for a moment after thus thinking. But if I were *not* discovered, might I not regain the blissful freedom for which I panted, laugh at the envious dupes of Milan, make myself as free as the eagle, and range the wide world with my adventurous heroine and my precious little ones. Excellent and invigorating thoughts! I began to work, having previously formed a bolder design; and after labouring, like Hercules, nearly thirty nights, unassisted by necessary implements, I made my way to the yard, which I can now enter by sinking a slight covering of earth.

"And now, Signor, for my grand project, which I have only distantly hinted to you. Dare you make a bold struggle for liberty?"

"I dare. But how to obtain it? the means?"

"By firing this infernal prison, and escaping in the tumult it will occasion."

"What! endanger the lives of those who are in confinement? of those who hope for pardon? of those to whom it may, even at the moment of your attempt, be actually granted? of those who have wives and little children waiting in tearful expectation at the grate, and perhaps looking for the husband and father while we are plotting their destruction?"

"No, no! my life on it that the gates and doors will be instantly thrown open, and that the emancipation will be general."

"If I thought so, indeed——"

"Assure yourself of it. Your scruples I would remove; yet may I perish if I do not reverence you for your humanity!"

"But how accomplish this? The fire, I apprehend, must be partial and confined; such an one, perhaps, as our gaoler will be able to smother with a blanket, or quench with a single bucket of water."

"There you are deceived; it shall be wide and terrible. I have already told you that my father was an extraordinary chemist; and I am the possessor of a secret art of conflagration, which nothing could ever tempt me to disclose. I will undertake to make a glorious blaze! What say you? Enterprise or death?"

"Enterprise! enterprise! I feel my heart glowing. To escape the monster that is preparing to gape for me, I will attempt any thing which you may boldly devise—I swear I will, rather than yield myself to his jaws, which never till now looked terrible."

"Bravo! if we do not succeed, we shall both die, but not upon a wheel! I have a dagger, and will use it; here is one for you, too, if you are inclined to apply it. Never stretch—stab rather than stretch! At the hour of twelve to-morrow night the struggle shall begin;—but let me disincumber you of these irons. Would I could twist them round the necks of some of the Milanese, and with them mount their carcases to gibbets nothing below the regions which the eagles, that might pull from their bones the bloated flesh which covers them, best love to shriek and wheel in!"

He began to file my fetters, and in the course of half an hour, owing to his extraordinary dexterity, I found myself unrestrained. I was cautioned by him, however, to affix the links properly in the morning, and also to be prepared for the visit of the gaoler.

"And now," said I, "inform me whether you know any thing

of the man whom you appear so willing to befriend? any thing respecting his condemnation—his crimes?"

"I have been informed that you are a murderer."

"And you still can serve me? still wish to preserve me?"

"I can—I do. When I first heard your accusation—"Let him go to the hell which he ought to burn in!" I exclaimed; "but when your conduct at your trial was represented to me, it pleased me; I pitied your situation, and admired your spirit; and recollecting my former impetuous speech, I not only blamed myself, but also cursed the rashness of my tongue. Afterwards, for I had curiosity to spur me on, I overheard your nightly lamentations, and scraps of a story, which I deemed to be truly lamentable, though I could possibly form no distinct ideas of it. Commiseration grew within me while you were perfectly a stranger to me; but when I looked upon your face, Signor, I could no longer believe that you were literally a murderer, or that you had, through mere savageness, stirred up the hot blood of a human creature with a cold and deliberate hand."

"Look at this picture," I said, taking the miniature of Rosolie from my bosom, and holding it near the lamp.

"Oh, how sweet! how lovely!" he exclaimed; "and whom does it resemble, Signor?"

"My wife; nor is there a line of flattery in it. She was indeed sweet! she was indeed lovely!"

"She *was!* Ah! then she is——"

"Dead! gone from me for ever! I would not speak of her before my judges; but you are a rare and uncommon friend, deserving of all confidence. You know that I killed a man of the name of Salvini; this ruffian defiled the temple of chastity; he bore my wife from me, not seduced, but forcibly deprived her of her honour! She sickened of grief, and died!"

"I cannot—dare I believe it?"

"By all that's holy and divine it is true! Now, without detailing any more of the horrid circumstance, tell me what the perpetrator of a crime like this deserved?"

"To be murdered cruelly; and, if it were possible, to be restored again to life, afterwards to suffer a thousand, nay, an hundred thousand lingering deaths. But you have chilled my blood. Unhappy man! miserable prisoner! my heart's stream is overflowing for your sufferings! but droop not—sink not at a moment like this. I must not suffer you wholly to unman me. Good night, my new acquaintance and confederate, for I have much business to perform before the morning, in which you can be of no service to me. My name is Pietro Arpino; and I am your friend, or may the clouds smother me! but if I lead you to liberty, Apollonia will be more entitled to your thanks than myself. Adieu! hold yourself in readiness to-morrow night, when Captivity shall growl for the loss of her victims, and the atmosphere of Milan be illuminated by the red flames bursting from this abominable pest-house."

He shook my hand, and descended.

I replaced the stone with great care, and then sat down in astonishment, almost doubting the reality of what had passed. The enterprise of Arpino I did not think would succeed; but I looked upon the dagger with pleasure, and treasured it as a friend that would snatch me from torture and disgrace.

On the character and principles of my fellow-prisoner I could not at that time think deeply; I saw enough of him, however, to excite curiosity and surprise, and he evidently was an extraordinary man. His person shewed a hero, for it was noble and beautiful; the vigour of his mind displayed itself conspicuously, and his firmness and courage I believed to be very great.

The dark hours went over, and on the following day I thought myself a successful hypocrite; for I assumed an habit of melancholy, and not only talked of my execution with dejection, but also, as evening drew on, begged that the Confessor might appear again the next morning, in order to take the burthen off my conscience, which I now found too dreadful and weighty. My commiserating gaoler withdrew. Collecting my papers, I put them in my bosom; and as the night further advanced, took off my chains, and watched for the appearance of Arpino.

At half past eleven he removed the stone, and giving me a squeeze, and whispering, "Silence," motioned me to follow him through the cavity, which I accordingly did, and almost immediately after found myself in his cell, where his secret apparatus and small instruments were placed.

"I have no time for talking," he said, in a low tone of voice; "I do not absolutely promise you liberty; but remember my present. If we succeed, we shall probably never meet again. Apollonia and my boys, my little unfledged eaglets, are removed to some considerable distance from Milan, and I shall strive to join them. Signor, you may want money; here is a purse for you, roughly, but freely given. The oil of compliments hangs not upon my tongue; and having been left to the tuition of Nature, the graces of speaking came not within the rules of my education. If you escape these walls, hide yourself in the suburbs till the morning, when you may easily pass the gates of the city; afterwards every thing will depend on your activity. But now to action; remain quiet till my return; if I am intercepted, God bless you!"

He collected his instruments; dipped several small balls of flax into a liquid; and putting his lanthorn under his clothes, disappeared.

I was disturbed by the most violent emotions, and in momentary expectation of seeing Arpino dragged back to his cell. After an absence, however, of nearly half an hour, he returned, and with exultation told me that the building was on fire in three different parts. The noise and confusion that soon followed, affirmed what he said to be true; the assistants of the prison were running disorderedly about the yard, and the bell announced the circumstance to the city.

Arpino took me by the arm, and soon after brought me into an open space, where the flames met my eye, and made me tremble at their violence and terrifying aspect. The tumult increased, and the noise of the populace, assembled before the prison, was very loud; but we thought it proper to retire a few minutes to our hiding-place till there were more people admitted within the walls. A considerable number was almost immediately after hurrying backward and forward, when we again ventured forth, and joined them, regardless of the probable consequences of our temerity. It was not a fit season to listen to the voice of Caution, and neither of us seemed inclined to attend to her.

I was soon separated from Arpino; and, expecting every moment to be arrested by the gaoler, or some other person, I grasped my dagger firmly; and after a short space of time, being seized with considerable force by the arm, I was applying the point of it to my breast.

"Roncorone! Roncorone!" cried Arpino.

"Is it you?" I said; "is it Arpino?"

"Are you mad?" he exclaimed, still grasping me, "are you mad? Here, take this bucket; follow bravely; imitate my actions, and repeat my words. Instant freedom, or instant death for me! Come on! come on!—— 'Fire! fire! water! water!'"

I kept at his heels, and made the same outcry as he did, in which we were joined by many more voices. We passed the gates!

"It is done! it is accomplished!" cried Arpino; "bold was the attempt, and glorious is its success! God bless you in every after-day! We must part instantly—God bless you!"

He broke from me; but I first grasped his hands, and let a tear of gratitude fall on them. What his fate afterwards was I know not; he however escaped from the city, on which I have grounded good hopes. According to his direction, I did not attempt to leave Milan till the break of day, when I passed the gates of the town, and walked undauntedly on, but still retaining the dagger of Arpino as a security against the power of any pursuers.

I had no means of disguising myself: at the first village I came to I purchased a horse (for the purse which Arpino had given me was plentifully stored), and mounting him, set off with speed, scarcely stopping an hour at any place till I reached the banks of the Lake of Maggiore, which I crossed, having previously disposed of my brute preserver.

I was happy to learn, by public report, that, though the greater part of the prison had been reduced by the flames, not a single person suffered in the conflagration. The names of Arpino and Roncorone were spoken of with terror; for the discovery of some of my friend's apparatus in his abandoned cell, and also of the passage that communicated to my dungeon, had betrayed to the keeper of the prison the principal actor and agent in this cunningly contrived business.

Large rewards, I heard, were offered for the apprehending of the incendiaries; when, in order to make greater my security, I procured a disguise, in which I journied on with caution, and at length reached the Valais; and, seeking a retired and unfrequented spot, became fearless of the hand of power, and unsuspecting of malice and stratagem.

What had I to do with men and society? Nothing. I had no mind to inform, no wit to charm, no suavity to please. On my own privacy I grounded my security; and callous as the depravity of the world had made my heart, still it would frequently soften at the simplicity and kindness of my untutored fellows.

* * * * * *

I have done:—God, whose spirits now whisper in the elements, knows what the sufferings of my soul have been, and what they now are. The total suppression of my breath will soon be effected, and the miseries of a condemned felon will speedily terminate. I, who once possessed bodily hardiness, am now enervated; sickness accompanies sorrow, and the fierceness of my mind is succeeded by dejection. Oh calamity! I have known enough of thee!

One of the honest natives has been endeavouring to win my favour, and he has succeeded; he wants to alleviate my distresses, to sooth my afflictions, and to make me an inmate of the little dwelling of which he is the master. He desires not to know my story; he sees that I am a creature of misery, and with tears in his eyes—(breeds such sympathy in cities?)—entreats me to live with him, and to enlarge his family of peace. To live! and, living, to be at peace! Ah! friend——

Good son of Nature! beneficent fellow-man! before I die, I will bless you a thousand and a thousand times. God protect the woman who sleeps within your arms, and prosper the children that have sucked at her breast! You have a little vineyard; may its fruit be tenfold! Envying not the sons of power, you look calmly on your spots of pasturage; gentle be the dews that descend on them! Long and prosperous days, a placid death, and a fair after-name be your reward, mild, charitable, and unoffending stranger!

* * * * * *

I became nearly two months ago a resident in the little farm; but I feel that I am about to leave it for ever. I shall be buried with decency: I have already chosen my resting place, and the children say that, if I die, "they will plant pretty flowers around my grave."

I crawled out yesterday, in order that the free air might blow upon me. An unexpected storm arose, but it was succeeded by a lovely calm;—the violence of the one I compared to the struggles of death; the serenity of the other to the state of immortality; and in the craving of my soul I stretched forth my almost fleshless arms to the cloud-enveloped spirit.

Alberti!—dear friend, I die!—Bless you and your wife!—Protect the orphan, and remember those who have, in some degree, soothed the agonies of the dying Roncorone. Take to your notice the friendly little boy whom I have mentioned before, and who saw me yesterday probably for the last time. Rosolie, ere the sun goes behind yon mountain, we shall surely meet. My eyes are misty— still your form is not imperfect.—Partner! wife! spirit!—Oh!——

Information to the Reader.

Roncorone never renewed his narrative; two days after this abrupt breaking-off, he purged his mind and body of their afflictions; and on the fifth subsequent to his death, the latter was given to the earth, under the direction of the humane rustic of the Valais, who afterwards took possession of the papers which the deceased had left behind him. This man, in the course of a few weeks, deposited the writings with a gentleman of Geneva, to whom he also gave the following short account of the unfortunate Venetian, and of his last moments.—

"His first appearance amongst us excited great curiosity, and in a short time his general manners and deportment created a considerable degree of terror in some of my neighbours, who distinguished him by the name of the "Mad Man of the Mountain." He at first took possession of a poor little hut that belonged to a vintager, of whom he purchased the scanty things which were in the house: his residence there, however, was only temporary; for the greater part of his time was spent in a rude cavern, of which the people of these parts have always been fearful. He was fond of the heights, and seldom came down to our valley, except to procure the few simple necessaries of life; and even then his words were very few, and also very strange.

"The first time I saw him, I both loved and pitied him. His face was beautiful, his person noble; and, ah, my God! when he was not wild, his sighs were so hollow, and his eyes so mournful, that I have often gone home to my family with a very heavy and afflicted heart.

"I once carried a small basket of fruit to him, and entreated him to accept of it;—he regarded me with fixed looks, which confused me, asking me at the same time whether I came to betray him; and then, as if recollecting himself, he took me by the hand, and thanked me for my simple present. I afterwards drew him to my little farm. Sometimes I could not understand his language, and I suspected him to be actually mad, as my neighbours reported him; but, at other periods, his words delighted my ear, and the soft tones of his voice seemed almost to draw my soul from me.

"My daughter Lisette and myself were the only persons with whom he would, for any length of time, patiently converse; and unhappy were we when we saw him roving, melancholy and heedless, over the brow of the mountain, or wandering, during a storm, through the lonely paths of the valley.

"Ah! how my heart has bled—how the eyes of Lisette have wept for the poor unhappy stranger, who at length seemed wholly to desert our house, and to hide himself from every eye! At the risk of raising his anger, we ventured to go to him: we found him pale and drooping; and, Oh God! the looks of famine were in his face. It was evident that he had long abstained from food. He was weak, thin, and sallow!

"As I suspected, he was at first displeased, and desired us to retire; but, endeavouring to make myself known to him, I urged him to go home, and to reside with me and Lisette till health and happiness should again return to him. He answered me with a look which, I must confess, half frightened me, and with a most unseasonable and very unnatural laugh; but he afterwards gave me a refusal, though he accepted of some provision that I had brought with me. About a fortnight after this shocking discovery,

I succeeded in getting him to my house; but I saw that his life was hastily fading.

"He was now less wild, but more melancholy; though he talked but little with us, his looks were generally kind and tender; and if we attempted to sooth or cheer him, he would water our hands with his bursts of tears. The marriage of my dear Lisette greatly affected him. On receiving the little bridal presents, his agony increased, and on hearing the strains of the flagelet, he hastily retired. Poor Lisette was sorry to see so much misery; she went after him, and, bursting into tears, asked whether he did not wish her happiness?—'God send it you till the day of your death!' he exclaimed, 'even till the last moment of your existence!'—He took her in his arms, kissed her, and then delivered her to her husband, who had followed her.

"In the evening I prevented him from committing an act of suicide; I arrested his uplifted arm, and in the name of God charged him to desist.—'God!' he repeated, 'God!'—He sunk on his knees, and the weapon with which he had armed himself, fell from his palsied hand.

"His time was but short after this occurrence; these arms supported him in death; these hands closed his eyes! That my heart was grieved is true, but unnecessary to repeat. He spoke of a friend, and of his wife—of his murdered wife! He seemed to hold strange dialogues with her, and talked of her as long as he could give motion to his lips. I know no more, and this I have found too sad for a weak old man. Though he be with God, I shall long mourn for him; humanity directed my actions towards the poor stranger, affection gave them force, and his grave must become an old object before it fails to excite sorrow."

The person to whom the peasant delivered the papers, was a man of understanding and compassion;—his first care was to forward intelligence of Roncorone's death to Alberti; who, on receiving it, hastened to Geneva, where he learned the wretched end of his best beloved friend, and almost brother, of whom he had endeavoured, during a space of several months, to obtain some information: but the narrative he received, convinced him that there were severer pangs for the heart than any which he had before been aware of.

On his return to Venice he removed many stigmas from the memory of Roncorone, and taught thousands to pity his fate who had hitherto cursed his crimes. Compassion no longer rested on the name of Salvini; infamy was attached to it; and his tomb at Venice, to which place his body had been conveyed from Milan with great funereal pomp, was regarded as the cave of a fiend, rather than as the resting-place of a Saint.

Some of the more rigid Seculars endeavoured to prove Alberti's unfortunate friend a criminal deserving of reprobation; but their malice was impotent, their arguments inconclusive, and their churlishness reviled at. Whoever mentioned the name of Roncorone, added, "Peace to his soul! peace to the ashes of his wife!"

FINIS.

CONTEMPORARY REVIEWS

ART. XII. *Mad Man of the Mountain; a Tale.* By Henry Summersett, Author of Probable Incidents, &c. 2 vols. Lane.[1]

THIS is a "tragic tale" of love and murder. To amuse, to excite an interest for fictitious misery, and to bend the passions at will, are not the only requisites of a novelist: instruction ought to flow from his pen, and his writings should display a warning to the vicious, and hold forth an encouraging beacon to the children of virtue.

Roncorone, the madman, the hero of the tale, is deeply injured by Salvini, a villain, without one shade of virtue in his composition. This villain receives the punishment due to his crimes; but he ought not to fall by the hand of private revenge: vengeance is not the attribute of man. The virtuous, the noble-minded Roncorone ought not to be the assassin of Salvini. Where the axe of the law cannot reach, the sword of eternal justice will extend, and man must not be the murderer of man.

This piece, though not a maiden effort, betrays several negligencies of style: repetitions, redundancies, and unmeasured periods, frequently obtrude themselves on the ear. The story, however, is not devoid of interest; and, at intervals, some promising traits of genius are exhibited.

The Mad Man of the Mountain: a Tale. By Henry Summersett, Author of Probable Incidents, &c. 2 vols. 12mo. 7s. sewed. Lane. 1799.[2]

Roncorone, a supposed Venetian, recounts in these volumes his adventures and misfortunes. He becomes enamoured of Rosolie, an amiable Florentine; but, as his father had been at variance with Salvini, the guardian of the young lady, he meets with

---

[1] *The Anti-Jacobin Review and Magazine*, vol. 6, p. 55 (1800).

[2] *The Critical Review, or, Annals of Literature*, vol. 29, p. 115 (1800).

some obstructions to his eager wishes. Rosolie is carried off by Salvini, whom, however, she firmly refuses to marry. Having conceived a strong affection for Roncorone, she resolves to take the first opportunity of escaping from her confinement. In the mean time, her lover, having procured some intelligence of the place of her abode, hastens in quest of her. In his way, he unknowingly rescues Salvini from the danger of being killed by a fall down a precipice; follows him to his house; and bears away Rosolie in triumph. He now espouses her, and passes some time in all the joys of chaste love. But his happiness is at length overwhelmed by the loss of his wife, who is seised in his absence, again confined by Salvini, and insidiously polluted by his adulterous lust. Her death being occasioned by this brutal treatment, the incensed husband murders Salvini, proclaims his guilt, and is condemned to death; but escapes from prison, and dies in exile.

Such is the substance of this novel. The character of the hero is drawn with spirit: that of his friend Alberti is amiable and interesting; and the language, though frequently inaccurate, is better than that of many of our recent novels. Upon the whole, we are of opinion that the author possesses some talents for fictitious narrative.